CHAINS OF THE SEA

BOOKS BY ROBERT SILVERBERG

Revolt on Alpha C
Lost Race of Mars
Time of the Great Freeze
Conquerors from the Darkness
Planet of Death
The Gate of Worlds
The Calibrated Alligator
Needle in a Timestack
To Open the Sky
Thorns
The Masks of Time
The Time Hoppers
Hawksbill Station
To Live Again
Recalled to Life
Starman's Quest
Tower of Glass
Earthmen and Strangers (*editor*)
Voyagers in Time (*editor*)
Men and Machines (*editor*)
Tomorrow's Worlds (*editor*)
Worlds of Maybe (*editor*)
Mind to Mind (*editor*)
The Science Fiction Bestiary (*editor*)
The Day the Sun Stood Still (*compiler*)
Beyond Control (*editor*)
Deep Space (*editor*)
Chains of the Sea (*compiler*)

CHAINS OF THE SEA

Three Original Novellas of Science Fiction

by

Geo. Alec Effinger
Gardner R. Dozois
Gordon Eklund

Edited and with an Introduction by Robert Silverberg

THOMAS NELSON INC.
Nashville   New York

No character in this book is intended to represent any actual person; all the incidents of the stories are entirely fictional in nature.

Introduction copyright © 1973 by Thomas Nelson Inc.
"And Us, Too, I Guess" copyright © 1973 by Geo. Alec Effinger
"Chains of the Sea" copyright © 1973 by Gardner R. Dozois
"The Shrine of Sebastian" copyright © 1973 by Gordon Eklund

All rights reserved under International and Pan-American Conventions. Published in Nashville, Tennessee, by Thomas Nelson Inc. and simultaneously in Don Mills, Ontario, by Thomas Nelson & Sons (Canada) Limited. Manufactured in the United States of America.

First edition

Library of Congress Cataloging in Publication Data

Effinger, George Alec.
  Chains of the sea.

  CONTENTS: Silverberg, R. Introduction.—Effinger, G. A. And us too, I guess.—Dozois, G. R. Chains of the sea.—Eklund, G. The shrine of Sebastian.
  1. Science fiction, American. 2. American fiction—20th century. I. Effinger, George Alec. And us, too, I guess. 1973. II. Dozois, Gardner R. Chains of the sea. 1973. III. Eklund, Gordon. The shrine of Sebastian. 1973. IV. Title.
PZ1.E36Ch [PS648.S3]   813'.0876   73-6444
ISBN 0-8407-6314-X

Table of Contents

Introduction Robert Silverberg	9
And Us, Too, I Guess Geo. Alec Effinger	11
Chains of the Sea Gardner R. Dozois	79
The Shrine of Sebastian Gordon Eklund	153

CHAINS OF THE SEA

Introduction

Science fiction is a field strangely characterized by periods of sudden creative ferment in which platoons of gifted new authors arrive all at once. One such period came just prior to World War II, when Theodore Sturgeon, Robert A. Heinlein, Isaac Asimov, A. E. van Vogt, Lester del Rey, and half a dozen other major writers made their debuts within the span of a year or two. About fifteen years later there was a similar upsurge that produced, all at once, such notable contributors to science fiction as Philip K. Dick, Robert Sheckley, Algis Budrys, Philip José Farmer, and Walter M. Miller, Jr. A decade after that—in the early 1960's—a third startling cluster of newcomers appeared simultaneously: Roger Zelazny, Samuel R. Delany, Joanna Russ, R. A. Lafferty, and Thomas Disch, among others. The process seems to be repeating itself in the 1970's, for, although it is a risky business to project the course of an entire career from the evidence of a few stories, one can already see that such new science-fiction writers as Ed Bryant, Gene Wolfe, Josephine Saxton, David Gerrold, and James Tiptree, Jr., are well on their way toward establishing themselves.

The present book is intended as a showcase for three of the most highly regarded of the newer writers: Geo. Alec Effinger, Gardner R. Dozois, and Gordon Eklund. All three belong unarguably to the literary generation of the 1970's. Aside from one story by Dozois that appeared in 1966, none of their work saw print professionally before 1970. They are still young: Eklund, the oldest, is several years short of thirty as I write this late in 1972. Yet they are no novices; as the evidence of this volume shows, their writing is skillful, evocative, thoughtful, occasionally profound. Despite the relative sparseness of their output to date, Effinger, Dozois, and Eklund have all been spoken of as potential winners of science fiction's highest awards for literary achievement, the Hugo and the Nebula, and no doubt will collect their share of these coveted trophies in the years ahead. The three short novels you are about to read are being published here for the first time anywhere, and represent, I think, a fair sampling of their authors' talents.

—Robert Silverberg

And Us, Too, I Guess
GEO. ALEC EFFINGER

Disaster stories have been commonplace in science fiction since the days of H. G. Wells. But usually the fictional catastrophes are spectacular noisy events—the continents are sundered by mighty earthquakes, a second deluge drowns the earth, the sun goes nova. Here Geo. Alec Effinger, one of the most highly regarded of science fiction's new generation of writers, gives us a quiet catastrophe, one which sneaks up subtly and obliquely on the world, a disaster that begins on a trivial scale and widens until it engulfs all of civilization. Effinger's first published stories appeared as recently as 1971, and only the following year his short story "All the Last Wars at Once" was a runner-up for the World Science Fiction Convention's Hugo award. His first novel, What Entropy Means to Me, *was published to warm critical acclaim in 1972. He and his wife currently live in Brooklyn.*

It was certainly a *quiet* cataclysm.

I remember very well how I reacted in its early days. Of course, it was by no means my first disaster; I had graduated from a good school where I received the best practical training, and afterward I had found a job with a well-known metropolitan research team. In the following months, during which I worked with some of the sharpest minds on the East Coast, I witnessed a small but decisive catastrophe. It ruined at least three lives, in addition to dissolving the research team and forever discouraging financial support in my own chosen field.

I was not deterred. It was necessary for me at that point to choose another field. No sooner had I reeducated myself and gathered the essential literature and equipment for my first solo experiments than the world at large was struck by a singular and devastating disaster. Again my work had to be postponed. I weathered the disturbance easily, but millions of people in the United States alone were permanently affected. My own assistant, Wagner of the hunched back, disappeared with my only set of keys, and I was forced for the third time to set out afresh.

I sought counsel from one of my former associates, Dr. Johnson. I felt that it would be foolish to continue entirely on my own, especially now that hardly anyone else could be at all useful. So I moved into Dr. Johnson's spacious apartments, and together we planned a good scientific project with plenty of chemicals and glassware, leaving the matter of goals and hypotheses for later. This partnership required that I leave my own headquarters in New York and take up residence in Cleveland, a city that I had always thought of as primarily for Ukrainians, hoodlums, and other nontechnical types. After a short time I grew more comfortable there, and our work began to lose the ugly dilettante aspects that new laboratories always seem to harbor.

Of course, with my luck, that's precisely when the cataclysm occurred. Or, to be more exact, when we (the scientific community) first began to acknowledge its existence, with whatever private misgivings. Not yet fully recovered from many superior twentieth-century disasters, the world was already beset by another. This one was not man-made; no, the proud scientific community could not take the slightest credit for it. Perhaps, I have come to think, perhaps that is the reason it took us all so many years to accept the truth. If only we had been granted a small part, a tiny creative task in the grand scheme of things, then the world and its inhabitants could have perished overnight without causing us an instant's regret.

But it's no use second-guessing the cosmos. Some ten years after my last meeting with Dr. Johnson I arrived by plane in Cleveland. My first impression of the area was unfavorable. Before I had even reacquired my luggage I had decided that it would be impossible to breathe the Ohio air. The temperature in mid-July was ninety-four degrees, and it was an hour and a half past midnight. The humidity was a Devonian ninety-two percent. I felt as if I had been squeezed from the plane into a huge stewpot at the simmer. My white labcoat seemed too heavy to carry, let alone wear. My legs and arms were unbearably weary, and if I had not seen Dr.

Johnson waiting for me at the gate, I might well have climbed back on the plane and gone home.

"Well, hello there, Dr. Davis," said Dr. Johnson, shaking my hand firmly.

"Hello, Dr. Johnson," I said. "It's nice of you to meet me."

"Not at all. Hot enough for you?"

I looked closely at my old friend. The Dr. Johnson I had known in my youth would never have permitted himself such a cliché. I had an inkling that I'd have to suffer more than merely the climate.

"Is it like this all the time?" I asked, forcing myself to proceed through the entire weather routine.

"No," said Dr. Johnson, pleased at my acquiescence, "sometimes it rains as well!" We both laughed briefly and walked in silence to his car. The parking lots were nearly deserted; the world's previous disasters could not yet be forgotten, and life continued on a much more distracted plane than I preferred.

Dr. Johnson had chosen a lovely old home in the Garden District. The former owners, like so many mere landlords, had been "incapacitated" by the catastrophe of the midseventies. So many of the old mansions along St. Charles Avenue had been deserted and taken over by the scientific community, alone among the city's residents still able to appreciate the neighborhood's charms. The two of us could barely fill a single chamber with our possessions, but we found ourselves masters of two dozen rooms. For the first time in my life I had a dormitory room of my own, plus a reading room, an office, two private baths, a private parlor for whatever visitors I might entertain, and a strange little closet-sized room at the end of a long corridor. There were no windows in this room and but the one door, and there was no clue as to what purpose the previous owners might have put it. Dr. Johnson suggested jokingly that I use it for a chapel, and at the time the idea was exquisitely foolish.

The entire back of the house, shaded by arching palm trees and great leafy shrubs I could not identify, was given over to our laboratories. The city of Cleveland was ours, as far as acquiring matériel was concerned; our only limits were placed by the other members of the scientific community with whom we competed. But the house was already admirably furnished. What appeared to be an old pantry had been converted into the main lab. Dr. Johnson had set it up along the lines we had learned both in school and during our mutual ill-fated project of a decade before. One wall had been covered with pine-plank shelves, which supported hundreds upon hundreds of little bottles of chemicals, all in alphabetical order. Their tiny red-and-white labels were peculiarly comforting. Along the opposite wall were cages of small animals, whose marble eyes followed us about in our splendid pursuits. Could they know what part they were to play in our work? No, of course not. But as Dr. Johnson could not avoid the effects of the earlier disaster, now speaking in annoyingly trite phrases, so, too, have I felt the most unclean anthropomorphic urges. It was not sympathy I knew for the unlucky beasts we kept, but it was another fell emotion with matching symptoms.

We worked long hours, feeling certain that someday we would find a method and an object. But none of that was important; it was the joy of pipettes and gram atoms that maintained us. Indeed, we did not recognize the hoped-for stimulus when it came. Surrounded by cataclysm, we labored blithely on.

One morning I came down from my rooms to find Dr. Johnson hard at work, although it was not yet noon. He had fed the fish in the tanks, had thrown some decomposing material into the terrariums, and was beginning to examine the wood shavings in the rodents' cages. He turned to me as I entered. His broad smile and the crackling freshness of his labcoat were all the reward I ever needed.

"Good morning, Dr. Davis," he said. "Your mollies have all kicked the bucket."

Yes, it was the beginning of a pleasantly restrained disaster.

Paul Moran searched his pockets for the house keys. "Come on, already," said Linda, his wife. It was very late, well after midnight, and her habitual mistrust of the city overruled any desire to placate Paul. At last he found the key chain and handed it to her; she took it nervously, glancing up and down the street to see if anyone lurked in the shadowed doorways.

"Go on, you're safe," said Paul. Then to himself he murmured, "I can't see why anybody'd bother, anyway." For all her insecurity, Linda took foolish chances. She hurried up the tenement steps while Paul unloaded the suitcases from the trunk of the car. He watched her for a few seconds, again thinking that someday a guy was going to be waiting for her inside the foyer. That would teach her, all right. Then maybe she wouldn't be in such a hurry to leave him with all the luggage. Linda opened the front door and disappeared for a moment while she unlocked the inner door. As Paul slammed the trunk lid closed, he heard her voice.

"Paul?" she said. He did not answer. "Paul? Are you all right?"

"What's the matter now?"

"The light in here's burned out. It's dark inside; I can't see."

Paul swore under his breath. "What do you want me to do about it?"

"Wait a minute," she said, her voice shaking audibly. "I'll come down and help you."

"Hallelujah," said Paul angrily. He waited on the sidewalk beside the suitcases. Linda stuck her head out of the front door, peering up and down the street once more. "It seems to be okay," said Paul cynically. "I mean, you only have to come about thirty feet, you know."

"I just want to be sure, that's all," she said harshly. "One day you're going to run out of luck, you're going to walk down some dark street not paying any attention, and you're going to end up with a Saturday-Night Special stuck in your back. Knowing you, you'd wind up getting your head blown off."

Paul didn't react the way she expected. She forgot that he'd heard all of this several times before. He just bent over and picked up two of the three suitcases. "Don't be so smug," he said at last. "I mean, where would that leave you?"

Linda had never considered that aspect before. She just stared at him. He smiled coldly and shoved the third suitcase toward her with his foot. Then he turned and carried his suitcases up the stairs to the door, never once looking around to see if she followed. Linda stood on the sidewalk for a short time, glaring angrily at his back, ignoring for the moment her nervousness on the night-shaded street. She started to shout something after him but stopped abruptly. Finally she just picked up the heavy bag and hurried up the stairs.

The Morans' apartment was on the fourth floor of the building. The light was out in the ground-floor foyer, and the first flight of stairs was hidden in a vague darkness. Paul considered how the city forced an unhealthy fear on its populace; passing beyond the inner door, Paul paused before he began climbing the stairs, suddenly feeling vulnerable and too much like an easy target. He readily granted what that notion implied: someone to take a sight on that target, waiting, quietly hiding in a second-floor ambush. Often the stairwell smelled of urine and vomit. More than once the Morans had returned home at night to find drunks and vagrants passed out on the narrow landings between floors.

Linda walked up the stairs behind Paul. She hated the building, but Paul insisted that they couldn't afford to move. As he struggled up the stairs with the luggage, Paul could hear her loud sighs. Tonight, fortunately for their ragged tempers, there were no foul-smelling bodies to block their way. At their door at last, he dropped the suitcases heavily; his deep, rapid breathing was intended to let Linda know that he hadn't enjoyed carrying the luggage. She was unlocking the door, but turned to look at her husband.

"All right," she said, "I'm proud of you for carrying those things up here. If it wasn't for you, we'd have to leave them out on the sidewalk all night. I think you're wonderful." She gave him a spiteful frown and finished opening the door.

"You know something, Linda?" said Paul, throwing the suitcases over the threshold into the kitchen of their apartment. "You know what? I think you're crazy. I think you're about the most frightened person I've ever known. It's almost sick, how scared you are all the time. It's not normal."

"Shut up, Paul," she said wearily. "It's time to go to sleep. We'll talk about my mental illness in the morning."

"That's just it, for God's sake. You're even too scared to talk about it. You're too scared to go on a trip out of the city, because the junkies will rob the apartment while you're gone. You're too scared to drive with me because I'll wrap the car around a telephone pole. You're too scared to stay here alone because some strange person will mug you. You're too scared to stay here with me because *I* might mug you."

"Have you ever listened to yourself?" asked Linda, already

in the bedroom undressing for bed, leaving the suitcases where they had fallen in the other room. "You want to talk about sick, you just listen to the crazy stuff that runs out of your own mouth."

"You're scared that I'm telling the truth, isn't that right?"

She peered around the doorway; Paul was lying on the couch, his shoes making grimy trails on the slipcover. "You want to know what I'm really afraid of, Paul?" she said. "I'm terrified that someday you *will* tell the truth. I mean, I can guess all the shady things you do behind my back. But I'm just scared that the true story will make my imagination look like a Disney movie, rated G. See, honey, I still love you. I give you the benefit of the doubt."

Paul didn't answer. He just sat up, clenching his fists angrily, composing several variations of his natural reply. But he wouldn't give her the satisfaction of making him shout at her. She smiled again, with even less affection, and disappeared into the bedroom. She continued undressing; at last he heard her turn down the bedspread and plump her pillow. Then he heard the creak of the bed's springs, and the click of the light switch. He sat on the couch for a while. In his furious, illogical mood he didn't want to follow her too soon. That would be a sign of weakness.

When he did decide to go to bed, about ten minutes later, he went into the bedroom and turned on the lights. Linda groaned sleepily, and Paul just sighed loudly.

"You're getting good at heaving those heavy breaths," said Linda, propping her head with one hand.

Paul hung his shirt in the closet. Without turning, he answered her. "My God, look who's complaining. The original martyr. What's the matter, does the light bother you? Don't try to tell me you were asleep already."

"You going to work tomorrow?" she asked.

And Us, Too, I Guess

"Of course I'm going to work," he said loudly. "Somebody has to around here. Just because you're having a baby doesn't make you the Great American Princess, you know."

"Because it's late. You'll never get up."

"You let *me* worry about that. I don't mind getting out of this house." After he finished undressing he went into the far corner of the bedroom, where two large tanks sat, their pumps humming, aerators bubbling, green lights shining and casting soft reflections on the dingy walls of the room. He switched off the green lamps first, then stooped down to check the equipment.

One tank was a normal large aquarium, holding fifty gallons. This was placed on a stand against the short wall, beneath a window that opened out on the street four stories below. The other arrangement was a group of three smaller tanks connected step-fashion, situated against one of the longer walls, opposite the bed. A ten-gallon tank was on a platform about chest level; a second was set against it about two feet lower, and a third rested on the floor. Water pumped up from the bottom tank caused the top aquarium to overflow into the second, which emptied into the lowest one, and so on in a cycle. This was Paul's breeding apparatus. Young fish born in the top tank were swept over the edge and into the second tank, thus protected from their cannibalistic parents, which were prevented from following by a strip of netting across the waterfall's lip. The babies eventually were swept again into the bottom tank when they came to the water's surface in search of food. Then the middle tank was sealed off, so a later brood of babies from the top tank would have the middle area without competition from the original fry.

"Feed them and come to bed already," said Linda. "God, you worry more over those fish than you do about me." Paul said nothing. Linda sighed. "Well, I knew that already. I mean, you worry more about them than you do about yourself, and *that's* crazy."

"My mollies are dead," said Paul quietly.

"That happens," said Linda, turning impatiently to face the other direction. "Mollies are not such a terrific long-term investment. So scoop out the dead ones and flush them down the toilet."

"Linda," said Paul softly, tensely, "they're *all* dead."

"All of them? For God's sake, you can't even be trusted with some fish. What kind of care did you take of them? I mean, God, what kind of trouble is a lousy fish?"

"They were all right Friday night when we left."

She turned to gaze at him, completely without sympathy. "You let all those fish die. First you move in that ridiculous tank and spend I don't know how much to fill it full of fish. Then you pay a hundred dollars for filters and pumps and all the junk the guy in the store said you needed. Then you build that ugly waterfall thing. And when you're all done, you let your fish die. You like looking at just the water and the green light? What's the matter, the fish get in the way?"

"They don't even look like they've been sick," said Paul. "No fungus or nothing. And it's silly to think the ones in the big tank would catch something from the mollies in the breeding tank."

"You left the heaters on too high. You boiled your own fish."

"The thermometers say eighty-one degrees. Perfect."

"You starved them."

"Don't be stupid," said Paul sourly.

Linda gave him a mocking laugh. "Me? I'm not the one who killed all your fish."

"I had two broods in the step tanks, plus the breeding

stock. I had over a hundred mollies in the big tank. Not a single one of them's still alive."

"It must look pretty sick, with all those dead fish floating around on the top of the water. Well, you don't need that pump noise no more. Turn it all off and go to sleep."

Paul stood slowly. He felt completely helpless. Linda was right, he *did* look foolish. There was nothing he could do to stop her gloating over his misfortune. If only he could just explain the thing to her without looking like a total idiot. But he had no idea why all the fish had died; in the morning he would test the water for acidity and salt content. Even so, he could only go to the store and buy more mollies. He didn't look forward to what Linda would say then.

It was a Sunday morning when Dr. Johnson gave me the bad news about my poor mollies. Of all the tropical specimens in our community tank, the mollies were my favorites. There was something about them that attracted me; the cherry barbs were far too ferocious, the black-lace angels too prim, the upside-down catfish, though comical, were still too gross. But the mollies held a simple charm. Flat, stark black they were, darting like scraps of shadow somehow let loose in the water. The males were so aggressively sexual that I always had to laugh. The poor exhausted females would try such maneuvers as hiding behind the plastic clamshell bubbler, but it never did any good. And the constant production of live young mollies appealed to my scientific senses—here was the Mystery of Life in miniature.

Except that now I had the Mystery of Death on my hands. I scooped out the bloated bodies of my former pets and examined them hurriedly. No white spots of ich, none of the telltale symptoms of velvet. I couldn't bear to look at them for long and ran downstairs to the unoccupied servants' quarters to flush the mollies down the loo. The toilet water swirled and roared, and the fish were swept along, tails pointing down toward their porcelain necropolis. I have to admit that I shuddered to see them go, imagining that in their dead, sodden movements I could recognize a sad farewell gesture.

The death of my mollies had upset me more than I had thought. I felt a sudden and very intense attack of anthropomorphism, and I hurried back to the lab. There was only one thing to do, and that was to replace the fish as soon as possible and forever after pretend that nothing had happened.

"Did you see them off all right?" asked kindly Dr. Johnson when I returned.

"Yes, indeed. Thank you."

"Why, you're as pale as a ghost," he said, with his customary concern. I started violently. Apparently my co-worker noticed, and apologized. "I'm sorry," he said. "I suppose I'll have to guard my tongue for a few days. I had no idea those mere fish meant so much to you."

"How could you know?" I said bitterly, immediately regretting my tone. "*You* care for nothing but those cold glass test tubes of yours."

"I'm sorry you feel that way," said Dr. Johnson, not taking offense. He must truly have understood the extent of my grief, and deep inside I was grateful for that. "Have I never shown you my own pets?" he asked.

"No, you have not."

"Then I must, tonight. They can be seen to best advantage after the moon has risen. It is nearly full, isn't it?" I only nodded, wondering what strange hobby he had adopted, and had successfully kept hidden from me.

"It is a strange thing," I said, feeling suddenly philosophic, a mood I had rarely entertained since achieving adulthood.

And Us, Too, I Guess

"I fail to understand how we, as members of the scientific community, can still be so upset by death. I mean, inasmuch as we are privy to so many of nature's quixotic secrets. Should we not, therefore, be more apt to accept death as just another universal constant, to be calculated and assessed, with no more emotional weight than, say, Boyle's law?"

"For me, at least, that *is* true," said Dr. Johnson with a faraway look in his eyes. "I cannot fear death. I am not repelled by its concrete signs. It is so common a phenomenon and, as you say, so universal that I tend to overlook it as I do the nightly progression of the stars. *Death, where is thy sting?*"

"The sting of Death is dying," I said quietly. Somehow I had to shake this illogical humor, in which I forced human traits on objects inanimate or even incorporeal. I had to change the subject. "What do you think of the Indians' chances this year?" I asked.

"Haven't followed them since 1954."

"It's very interesting lately," I said nervously. "With most of the country's athletes still suffering from the old disasters, the ball clubs have signed many well-known scientists to play."

Dr. Johnson turned to look at me thoughtfully. "I wonder," he said, and then fell silent again.

"Did you like the Indians?" I asked sadly.

"They died like flies in the mid-seventies. I saw a bunch of dead Indians in Arizona. Just lying around, stacked like cordwood. It's not true what they say about dead Indians vis-à-vis good ones. You have to learn which generalities you can trust."

And there we were, talking about death again. This new catastrophe, of which the death of the mollies was the first indication, was a lot more drawn out than the usual. Almost as if it wanted to inflict every last bit of mental torture before it began the physical.

I will cease calling my phrases "anthropomorphic." From now on I think I'll just say "romantic." Nowadays, who cares?

The morning after the loss of his fish, Paul arrived at the factory at nine o'clock sharp. His foreman met him in the coatroom. Paul nodded and hung his jacket in his locker. The sight of Kibling waiting by the bank of dark-green lockers annoyed Paul. The foreman couldn't wait for five minutes while Paul punched in. The company had to drain every penny's worth of work out of its employees.

The Jennings Manufacturing Corporation paid Paul three and a half dollars an hour to do meaningless tasks. At least, the succession of chores never seemed to him to have any connection. Today, more concerned with the mollies' mysterious accident, he was in no mood to be bullied by his employers.

"Morning, Moran," said Kibling. "Here, I got a job for you."

"You know something, Gary?" said Paul, grinning so Kibling might think that he was only joking. "You know, you *always* got a job for me. It never fails. I come in on time every morning, and every morning you sure as sunshine got some dumb-ass job for me."

Kibling did not think that Paul was joking. He just sucked his teeth for a few seconds. "Any time, Moran," he said at last. "Any time you don't want the job, well, we got enough guys waiting outside."

"I wasn't serious, Gary," said Paul. "It's like a game. I never know what I'm supposed to do from one day to another."

"Try to think of that as an extra."

"Great. What's today? Front panels again?"

Kibling shook his head. "No, you didn't do too good on them last time. You're going to do the oven this morning. Get these plates done by lunch and I'll put you on subassembly for the afternoon."

Paul frowned and took the small, odd-shaped pieces of alloy steel from the foreman. The oven was the worst of his several chores. Kibling must have understood that; Paul got the assignment only once or twice a month. He had to toss three or four of the metal sheets into a small but very hot furnace. Every ninety seconds he reached into that glowing pit with a long-handled shovel and flipped them. He let them bake according to a standard schedule. When he removed them he put them aside to cool, dipped them in a strong-smelling chemical bath, knocked the coating of ash off as best he could, and sent the package on to Quality Control. Then he began all over, pitching another three or four sheets into the kiln.

The job gave him a lot of time to think. That was by far the worst part. Every word that Linda had spoken the night before came back to him, and he was infuriated all over again. He remembered his own replies without pleasure. While he waited for the steel pieces to cook, he thought up better answers. He knew what he'd say to her tonight, if she started that same argument.

After Linda, he thought about his fish. By lunchtime he had stopped worrying about them. The situation didn't allow that; there was nothing to be gained by regretting the waste. Black mollies were cheap enough. Wholesale, he could get a good pair of them for about a quarter. Ten females, three or four good, strong males, and he'd have all the dead fish replaced in six to eight weeks. No, it was just the surprise of seeing them all dead that had upset him the night before.

He couldn't summon up the same emotion now, twelve hours later. And, no doubt, Linda would try to run the matter into the ground when he came home. He changed his mind: rather than fight, he'd have to ignore her.

Paul decided to get the new mollies after work. Then he wouldn't have to go straight home, and when he did, he'd have something to occupy him. Even cleaning four tanks and changing the water was better than hearing Linda's new problems. Paul watched the clock all afternoon, and punched out on the time clock precisely at five. The subway was uncomfortably crowded with rush-hour commuters, but Paul just closed his eyes and disregarded them. They were all a little like Linda, in their pushing and shrieking. If they were quieter, more subtly insistent, then they might have infuriated him. But Paul had a great deal of practice in shutting irritations out of his mind.

The fish store was not just a neighborhood pet shop. It had no large front windows filled with romping puppies to lure the sentimental passerby. The store dealt only in aquariums, equipment suited to the needs of the fish-raising hobbyist, and the fish themselves. In the past few months Paul had become well known in the establishment, so that the proprietor had offered to buy Paul's growing supply of mollies. Paul had agreed to accept payment lower than the store paid to its regular distributor. But now, with the demise of all of Paul's salable goods plus the breeding stock, he was back in the role of customer. No longer did he *belong*, in the sense of being a fellow breeder, a colleague in the small field of tropical-fish raising. Now he was just a man with eighty gallons of bubbling water and no fish.

"Mr. Moran!" said Moss, the store's night manager. "Haven't seen you in a couple of weeks. Have you thought about our offer?"

Paul nodded glumly. "Yeah," he said, "but the deal will have to wait. I had some kind of accident or something. I was away for the weekend, and last night when I got home every molly I had was dead."

Moss looked surprised. "You had quite a few, I know. It sounds like you had some kind of plague."

"I doubt it. The fish were in four separate tanks, one big one and the step-breeder. I can't figure it out. There wasn't enough time for them all to catch sick and die."

"No," said Moss thoughtfully, "I didn't really mean that. It would have to be a mechanical failure, or a sudden change in pH or temperature."

"That was what I figured, too," said Paul, "but I checked all that as carefully as I could. The pH was perfect, the salt was as high as it's supposed to be, the temperature was right on eighty-one, where it's always been. Even if the pump had quit, there wasn't enough time for the water to go bad. I know there *wasn't* a mechanical failure."

"Have you ever had a pandemic infection before?" asked Moss.

"Huh?"

"You know, something gets in and kills a few fish. Then in a couple of weeks they're *all* dead."

"No," said Paul, discouraged that the expert in the store wasn't being more helpful. "Anyway, you'd have to be pretty careless to let something like that happen."

"A lot of people are that careless," said Moss. "We build our profits on them."

"This was just over the weekend," said Paul impatiently.

"I don't know, then," said Moss. "So what do you want, more breeding stock?"

"Yeah. I guess I'll just have to start from scratch." Paul followed Moss toward the back of the store, where the walls were lined with scores of small tanks, each containing a different variety of tropical fish. When they got to the three tanks of black mollies, Moss stopped abruptly and stared. Every molly in the store was dead. "You ought to keep a closer watch on your tanks," said Paul. "That sure won't impress a new customer."

"I just started work about fifteen minutes ago," said Moss. "Let me see if any of the day staff knows anything about this." Moss went to the front of the store to question the young man who worked behind the cash register. Paul stayed behind and examined the tanks of dead mollies. There was something chilling about them, beyond the mere coincidence. Whenever a single fish had died in Paul's tank, he scooped it out with the long-handled net and ran with it to the toilet, where he flushed the limp, dead thing out of his life. But the sight of so many fish lying on the bottom or floating upside down forced the idea of death into his consciousness.

While Moss was checking with his employee, Paul tried to see if the store's mollies resembled his own dead fish. The common diseases to which mollies were susceptible were obvious to the knowledgeable observer. Mollies are small fish, smaller than goldfish but larger than guppies. They come in many varieties and many colors, but the most popular strain is the pure black. The black molly is a dramatic addition to a community tank; the jet-black color is an exciting contrast to the many luminescent hues of other tropical fish, and mollies can be bred to develop fantastic fin and tail forms. They are usually hardy fish, prolific breeders in captivity, and thus make ideal pets for both the specialist and the casual hobbyist.

The most hazardous illness is ich, a parasitical disease that shows up as small white specks against the pure-black body. The disease is extremely contagious, and a tankful of mollies can be wiped out in a matter of days if no steps are taken to check it. Its presence generally means that the water doesn't contain enough salt, as mollies like their water a little brinier than most other tropicals. Without the salt, their protective coating of slimy film is easily penetrated. But there was no sign of this disease, neither on Paul's dead fish nor on the store's. Looking closer, he could see no symptom of mollie velvet or any other sickness with which he was familiar.

"Mr. Moran?" said Moss. Paul turned around, startled. "I asked some of the day staff, and they knew that the mollies had died. Miele said they were already dead when he checked them first thing this morning. But as you can see, there aren't any traces of disease. The tanks were left for me to examine, but I don't think I'll have any more success diagnosing ours than I had with yours."

"They *are* a lot like my mollies," said Paul tonelessly.

"Yes, of course," said Moss, watching Paul uneasily, unwilling to agree that there might be some connection. "Of course, you purchased your original stock from us, but I don't think we can be held responsible."

"It's certainly comforting to know that it isn't just the little people who can be careless." Moss frowned but did not answer. Paul shook his head, turned, and left the store.

The ride home was as crowded as the ride to the fish store had been. But, he told himself, now he had the rather sad consolation that Linda wouldn't be able to mock him for buying several dollars' worth of new mollies. Right after supper he would go into the bedroom and begin the arduous job of cleaning and sterilizing the tanks.

The meal with his wife passed silently, tensely. Linda had made spaghetti again, finding time in her long, lonely day only to boil water and warm a jar of commercial sauce. Paul was very angry; he came home to spaghetti at least three times a week. As soon as he had finished eating, Paul left the table and disappeared into the bedroom. Half an hour later Linda came in to see what he was doing.

"You taking all those sickening fish out of the tank now?" she asked.

Paul turned around slowly and regarded her for several seconds. "You want me to leave them here for you to look at?" he said quietly.

"Oh, don't be like that," she said, tossing a dish towel over her shoulder. "Just don't drop any on the rug. And watch that you don't splash that filthy water around my bedroom. Are you going to get rid of those tanks now?"

Paul turned back to his work. "Naw," he muttered. "Going to get some more."

"Huh?"

"I said I'm going to order some new mollies."

"So they can die off, too, and waste more money?"

Paul scooped the last of the dead mollies from the large fifty-gallon tank. He picked up the pot that held the others and carried it into the kitchen. As he passed Linda, she backed away, a disgusted expression on her face. "Listen," he said, dumping the fish into the garbage bag, "I went to the fish place after work. All of *their* mollies died last weekend, too. And I bought mine from them, so it can't be my fault. Your trouble is you're too quick to make me look like a fool. I'm not as dumb as you think I am."

Linda went back to the sinkful of dishes. "Just take that garbage downstairs before you do anything else. Use some common sense, for heaven's sake."

That night, when the large tank and the step-breeder stood empty and clean, after the filters and air lines had been washed and sterilized, Paul decided to order some breeding stock from a supplier in Connecticut. He wrote a letter, asking the price for ten females and four males. Several days later he received a reply, and the situation took a stranger shape. The letter said:

> We here at G & G appreciate your interest, but regret to say that your order cannot be filled at this time. Our entire stock of *Mollienisia sphenops* perished early this week, and we have been unable to receive replacements from our usual sources. I would normally suggest that you try our competitors, but curiously they have all experienced the same misfortune.
> Hoping to be of more service in the future, I remain,
>
> > Very truly yours,
> >
> > Walter G. Gretne
> > G & G Aquarium Supply

Paul was confused. It was as if somebody were making it hard for him to refill his tanks. Linda would say that they were trying to tell him something. But Linda only believed in fate or God when something bad happened to someone she knew. He decided not to mention the letter at all and, in fact, to seem to forget all about mollies until he could locate a source of healthy fish.

The next day, Sunday, he ignored Linda's pointed questions about all the expensive equipment going to waste in the bedroom. He didn't want to think about it. It was his weekend, and he wanted to relax. The Sunday paper was split up all over the house. Paul had the baseball news with him in the bathroom. The remaining sections were divided among the other rooms, and Linda had the television section with her in the bedroom. When Paul had finished with the sports, he stuck his head around the corner of the bedroom. "You got the movie section in here?"

Linda lay on the bed, the tiny portable television next to her. She was listening to an old Alan Ladd film while she read the paper. "Yeah," she said, "but I'm going to look at it next. You can have the TV section."

"I don't want the TV section," he said impatiently.

"There's something in it that might interest you." She pulled the first and last pages off the section, further separating the newspaper. She handed the sheet to Paul. "Something about your stupid fish," she said.

Paul searched the pages for the article she meant. At last he found it, a small piece several lines long, stuck in as a filler at the foot of a column. It said, rather tersely, that scientists had noted that no members of the species *Mollienisia sphenops* could be found alive in the United States, or even at their natural breeding grounds in the waters around the Yucatán Peninsula and Guatemala. The paper said that the scientists were puzzled.

The next few days were among the most bewildering of my somewhat eventful life. The situation certainly appeared simple enough on the surface: my mollies had died, I had to get new ones, and I had difficulty locating healthy specimens in Cleveland. At first Dr. Johnson took little more than amused interest in my problem. You must remember that at this time we had no idea of the magnitude of the circumstances; we were ignorantly working away on our mice and rabbits, frogs and flies. We gave no thought for anything more serious than the weekly party with our colleagues or our lapsed subscriptions to various scientific journals. Often we went down to watch the sun set over the river or rise

And Us, Too, I Guess

over the lake, while around us the universe prepared its next terrible blow.

The day after the mollies died, Monday, I was busy all afternoon helping Dr. Johnson construct a towering, brittle webwork of glassware. It was supported by heavy black iron stands at critical points. Flasks were the major component, a strong, optimistic theme that was typical of my friend. Connecting them were dozens and dozens of long glass arteries. Where some members of the scientific community in Cleveland would, I'm sure, have been satisfied to remain with the straight, purely functional tubes, Dr. Johnson did not hesitate to introduce long, delicate bends or even rude petcocks. The levels at which the flasks stood were pleasingly random, another nontechnical touch that made Dr. Johnson's creations superior to those of his contemporaries. Certain obscure, baroquely contorted pieces of glassware punctuated the whole structure, adding definite statements of progress and enterprise among the soothing chords. As a minor helper to the construction, I could only watch with amazement and respect as Dr. Johnson added one faultless detail after another.

By evening the thing was completed. Dr. Johnson ceremoniously made each of us a champagne cocktail, and we toasted his new work. Then I snapped the switch, killing the lights in the auxiliary lab; meanwhile Dr. Johnson had moved to his new *parvum opus*. He connected a plug from a strange piece of apparatus to a long extension cord. A bright-blue spark began to flick among the towers and tiny catwalks of glass. The eerie light cast hideous shadows in the room, and I was seized with a new, almost unpleasant awe for Dr. Johnson and his creative faculties. But no sooner had I begun to creep forward for a better view than he turned the lights back on in the room. "Enough," he said, waving his hand impatiently. "It does not work."

"It's beautiful!" I said, dismayed by the fury of his passion.

"It is not," he said. "It is clumsy. Lopsided, unbalanced. Tomorrow I will destroy it."

"You can't, my friend," I said, genuinely horrified. "You're too critical of your achievements."

He studied me for a few seconds, his expression contorted by emotions I fear I shall never experience. "What can you know of an artist's pain?" he asked. He was right, of course; in the morning I helped him destroy it.

His problems, his creative agonizing helped me to forget my own meager troubles. Monday had sped by with the assembling of his glass masterpiece; Tuesday saw its slow, tedious dismantling. I was greatly fatigued that night, as it was I who had to climb high to loosen flasks and tubes and Fleischer retorts. Dr. Johnson preferred to stand by and direct me; I did not think he was remiss in not helping me more actively. I recognized that he was, in his peculiar way, a genius; people of that caliber are entitled to a few eccentricities.

So, then, it was Wednesday before I was able to get around to calling at the few remaining pet stores in the Cleveland area. I tried one on Melpomene Street first of all, because that store had always given us a good deal on shredded lettuce and dead mice, food for various laboratory animals. Old Miss Fry told me tearfully that all *her* black mollies had died Sunday, too. I remarked on the sad coincidence, and how cheap it seemed of nature to merely duplicate her efforts in our separate aquariums. Miss Fry looked at me blankly, not comprehending my romantic notion, and I explained that I thought that possibly "something was going around." She laughed, and I tried another store. This one, on Terpsichore Street, not far from Miss Fry's, had abominable-quality fish but very nice "extras." I had spent a good deal of our budget on such things as marbles, painted glass bridges for the catfish to rest under, bubbling skin divers, bubbling sunken wrecks, bubbling treasure chests, and bubbling mermaids. I had even purchased as a joke a couple of dozen plastic fish; these had thin, almost invisible strings with weights tied to the ends. I buried the weights in the sand of one aquarium, and the fish hung suspended, always at one place. Though they never moved, I don't believe Dr. Johnson ever noticed that they weren't real fish. He didn't take to my pets as much as I; I think he even resented the amount of money I spent to keep them happy.

Anyway, I was told in the second shop that all their mollies had died the previous Sunday. I felt a peculiar thrill of fear. I had often felt that thrill before, and so I was not particularly interested now. But I thought that Dr. Johnson, at least, and possibly the entire scientific community might be intrigued by this gloomy turn of events. There might even be a project worth pursuing by some crew-cut statistician.

I followed St. Charles farther toward the downtown area, hitting all the pet shops I knew. In each, the story was the same: every black molly in Cleveland had died spontaneously, sometime Sunday afternoon. I was becoming increasingly tired, as well as fascinated by the latent horror of the situation. I decided to try one last place, a dirty establishment in the Quarter. I rarely had occasion to travel into that neighborhood, because its residents were some of the more lunatic of the city's population, all entirely overcome by the old disaster of several years ago. But I had little choice now; my scientific curiosity, sluggish to arouse at best, was now at last piqued and would not allow me to halt before some slight explanation might be had. I thought immediately of a virus, but dismissed the idea as unworthy.

I entered the sordid little shop unenthusiastically. The owner, one Mr. de Crout, hurried to meet me at the door.

"Have you any mollies?" I asked, wasting little time.

"No, they're all dead," he said, turning to retrace his steps to the back of the store and his small television.

I took the St. Charles streetcar home and told Dr. Johnson all about my day's adventure. As I foresaw, he was deeply concerned. From that time on he assumed control of the investigation, leaving me with a good deal of time to practice my own glassware sculpture. I had at last built something that I felt approached his own triumph of Monday, when he burst into the room, his face flushed and his labcoat torn at one shoulder. He seemed not to notice.

"I have news!" he cried.

"Look at this," I said.

"Never mind, we don't have time for such as that. Every molly in the city has been accounted for, and they're all dead. Every molly in the country is dead as well; I have proof." Here he waved a sheaf of telegrams. Each one was a molly count of a particular segment of the United States. Dr. Johnson had organized the fact-finding operation well. His efficient handling of the matter made me see him in a new light; he was, beyond doubt, my superior in such things. "Further," he said, his voice rising to unaccustomed levels of pitch and volume, "there is not to be found a single living molly in all of the coastal waters of the Yucatán or Guatemala, or the Gulf of Mexico, or Florida, their natural breeding grounds."

I stared at him. The thing was monstrous. "What do you make of it?" I asked.

"What else?" he asked, throwing the papers at me impatiently. I laughed with delight. "The species is done for," he said, pacing agitatedly. "I believe that an entire variety of animal life has become extinct, within the unbelievably short time span of a single day."

"Do you know what you suggest?" I said, with the necessary scientific skepticism.

"Yes," he said tiredly. "The world will think me mad, but I have done my duty."

"You mean—"

"I have informed the newspapers."

Then he *was* serious. I considered the problem for a moment. Before I could begin to sort my thoughts, I got the old familiar tingle: disaster! I smelled a disaster brewing, but it was too early to dig up more facts. I would have to wait.

"Sorry, old friend," he said, jerking me from my reveries with a slap on the shoulder. "I know those little buggers meant the world to you. You'll just have to get on without them. Switch your allegiance, as it were. Why not guppies, eh? Or something else altogether. Get out of the fish line." I could see that he was right. I said nothing, though, letting him feel sorry for me. I turned and took up my sculpture where I had stopped.

An hour later he came running into the room all over again. This time I truthfully saw tears on his cheeks, the only time I have known him to weep alone. "They're dead!" he whispered hoarsely. "All of them! Dead!"

"I know," I said with some irritation.

"No, you don't understand," he said, grabbing the sleeve of my labcoat. "My beautiful pets! They're all dead!"

Well, now, I remember thinking that at last I'd get to see his pets, which he had so carefully guarded from the view of the world at large. Even *I* had never seen them; I did not know so much as what they were, except dead. Now my instinctive tingle let me know: a new and perilous phase was beginning.

There was a great movie on at eleven thirty. The paper gave it only two stars; Paul had seen the film in a theater when it first came out, and he remembered that it was much better than that. The movie was one of Philip Gatelin's last, and Linda had never been one of his fans. She wanted to watch one of the talk shows. But finally she sighed loudly, admitting defeat and accepting the lesser comforts of martyrdom. Paul changed the channel; the news was still on.

"Move that over, will you?" said Linda, pushing the small television set toward her husband. "Maybe I'll just go to sleep."

"Why don't you do that?" asked Paul. "At least shut up."

"Shut up yourself. I want to hear the weather."

Before the local weather report, however, they had to watch a filmed interview prepared by the network. This spot, near the end of the newscast, was usually reserved for the day's absurd happenings, or for quick glimpses of the nation's crazier citizens. It was obviously in this spirit that the network newsman had been sent on his assignment.

"Hello," he said, "this is Bob Dunne, NBC News in Romisch, Iowa. I'm standing outside the Pany Institute of Wentell Agricultural College. With me is Dr. Kyril Levy, head of the Institute and an expert in pharmacological botany. Dr. Levy has made a rather startling discovery but, like many of his scientific predecessors, he's having a difficult time convincing his colleagues. But I'll let him describe his findings himself. Dr. Levy, just what is happening here in peaceful Romisch?"

Levy was short and gaunt, middle-aged, his hair thinning prematurely, his stooped shoulders accentuated by the rumpled white labcoat he wore. He took a deep breath and began. "It's not just here in Romisch, Bob. That's the point of the whole matter. No, we're all faced with the same problem, every one of us here in the United States and abroad."

Dunne didn't get any information at all with his first question. He tried again. "Could you summarize that problem for our viewers?"

"Certainly, Bob. My primary experiments here at the Institute concern the applications of dexterity equivalencies in the production of larger-yield money crops. For my purposes, I've been using a certain type of fungus. The experiments are general enough so that the results may be extended to include most other common money crops; the fungus has the added advantage of economy of cultivating area and growing season. The fungus, called by its Latin name, *Polyporus gugliemii*, is a pinkish-white, leathery growth that is found only on the trunks and limbs of a particular kind of Spanish catalpa.

"My experiments were coming along well, and last week I had reached what I estimated to be the midpoint of the program. So you can imagine how disappointed I was when I learned that every single *gugliemii* had died in the space of eighteen hours."

Dunne regained the initiative, looking into the camera with an amused but patient expression. He was humoring the scientist for the sake of a few laughs. "I can imagine that would be a horrible sight," he said.

"Yes, indeed," said Levy. "When they die, their stalks go limp. The weight of the huge caps bends them over. *Gug-*

liemii are very bright orange on the underside, you know, with dark brown speckles. Well, it was just awful. All those poor orange corpses staring at me."

"And did you try to replace them?"

"Of course. I called one of my colleagues in Wachnough immediately. I had introduced him to the *gugliemii* at last year's convention. Anyway, he said that all of his had died under the same inexplicable circumstances."

"Admittedly," said Dunne, "the fate of Dr. Levy's mushrooms has little personal meaning for the average man in the street. But what makes the mystery unusual, if only from a specialist's point of view, is the fact that apparently every one of those mushrooms in the world is now dead. Dr. Levy has done extensive research in the short time since his own mushrooms died, and has been unable to find any. So check your Spanish catalpas. If you find a pinkish-white thing growing there, let Dr. Levy know. If not, well, maybe the world will have to get along without the *Poly—*"

"*Polyporus gugliemii.*"

"Thank you, Dr. Levy," said Dunne, with an indulgent laugh. "This is Bob Dunne, NBC News, Wentell College, Romisch, Iowa."

Back with the local station, the announcer made a rude remark and introduced the weatherman. Paul watched the set silently, thinking. Linda had said nothing during the filmed interview, probably wondering why the network had invested so much money in such a dumb story. Who would miss a lousy mushroom? It was probably poisonous anyway.

"I know how he feels," said Paul.

"Huh? What do you mean?"

"I said, I know how he feels. That guy in Iowa. All his mushrooms died."

Linda turned around and propped herself on one elbow.

"You don't know what you're talking about," she said. "He's a scientist. His mushrooms meant something. Maybe he was working on something important. Your cruddy fish weren't important."

"Not to you, they weren't," said Paul coldly.

"You're doggone right, they weren't. They all dying may be the best thing that ever happened to you. Maybe you'll open your eyes. Now you can get into something useful, if you're smart."

"It's scary," said Paul, once more grateful to be able to shut his wife's words out of his mind. "First, all the mollies in the world die. All at once. Then these mushrooms."

"They both start with *m*," said Linda.

"What does that mean?"

"Maybe Morans are next." She laughed at herself and turned around again to go to sleep.

Paul stared at her back. "I wouldn't joke about it," he said thoughtfully.

Several days passed in their usual unfulfilling way. Paul thought no more about the scientist's fungi; he remembered the mollies every time he saw the abandoned tanks in the bedroom. Once or twice a day he would realize, as though for the first time, that he'd never see a molly again. Eventually he grew bored and sold the step-breeder, the large tank, and all the equipment back to the Fish Store. Linda laughed and said, "I told you so."

Paul's life was so carefully regulated that he never examined the events of the week more closely. His job continued the same, day after day; he thought the same things at the same times, admitting his frustration but lacking the imagination to battle it. His relationship with Linda, though not ideal, at least had the virtue of being constant. He could look forward to years of the same, never a misstep from her, never a fall from the peculiar grace they had arranged. And, too, he would be faithful. He had enough inclination to the contrary—surely no one could fault him for looking at other women—but his minor existence sapped whatever energy he might have had. He just couldn't be bothered.

Days and weeks later, toward the middle of September, an article in the newspaper caught his attention and brought back the short-lived feeling of fear. Paul welcomed it; even a change to impersonal terror would be a relief from the flat monotony he had built with Linda.

The article reviewed a speech given by Dr. Bertram Waters of Ivy University. Speaking before a meeting of the American Plasmonics Society, Dr. Waters revealed the results of a month-long survey conducted by himself with the aid of the North American Biological Research Association. Although biology was not Dr. Waters' own field, and although his audience had come hoping to hear of his recent work in the area of applied plasmonics, his lecture caused a great deal of excitement.

"We are right this minute caught in the midst of an unimaginable catastrophe," said Dr. Waters. "Even as we sit here, the forces of nature, those immutable ordinances by which we shape our lives, conspire to spell our doom. But because the calamity is a slow one, because it operates on a large scale, striking down victims in isolated places around the globe, we may be inclined to dismiss its effects on ourselves as negligible. That would be a suicidal error.

"A few weeks ago, every member of the species *Mollienisia sphenops* was killed by some unknown agent, no matter where in the world the fish might have been. This event caused some little comment but was quickly forgotten, except by breeders of tropical fish. A short time later, every specimen of the fungus *Polyporus gugliemii* was noted to have perished.

And Us, Too, I Guess

Since then, with the aid of NABRA, I have made a list of other species which have become extinct, suddenly and with no apparent—let me amend that: no *rational*—reason. Yes, there are other species. This list has been prepared carefully; all the extensive resources of NABRA have been employed to check it thoroughly, and I have every confidence in its accuracy. There are twelve other species, eight members of the plant kingdom, four of the animal kingdom, which no one here will ever see alive in nature again. Most of them, of course, will hardly be missed by the common man. Three of the four animals, for instance, were insects, tiny creatures barely distinguishable except by an expert.

"But that is not the point. One of the plants was noted by a botanist in Switzerland to have gone out of existence several years ago, 'seemingly overnight.' Other researchers have remarked on similar occurrences, some of which are still being investigated and may eventually be added to the list. What does this mean? Here is my theory, one which is highly speculative and will prove highly unpopular. Some of you will brand me a mad romantic, or worse. Nevertheless, in my opinion this is what the evidence points to.

"Who knows how many separate species of animal and plant life are on the earth today? The total must run into the trillions. The catalogued varieties alone are far too numerous for any man to comprehend. If only one species disappeared each day, beginning with the birth of Christ, no, the appearance of thinking man, no, even more, *the creation of the world*—it is possible that we would scarcely have noticed the difference. So many unclassified insects, bacteria, microbes, sea creatures exist that man can hardly hope even to name them all.

"I think that whatever put us here, all of us, man and animal and plant alike, is calling us home. One by one. The black mollies have been called. And the *gugliemii* fungus. And the *echai* fly. And who knows how many others over the course of eons? And who knows which will be next? We cannot even know how often this strange selection takes place."

The article went on at greater length, giving the conclusion of Waters' speech and the outraged reaction of his audience. But Paul was oddly contented. Perhaps it was only the idea that there might be, after all, some sort of *plan*, however gruesome and arbitrary it seemed. He looked into the kitchen, where Linda was making supper. Suddenly he felt a surge of affection for her, something that hadn't happened since shortly after their marriage. Paul wondered how long the feeling would last; he figured sadly that it would take more than a few mollies and a fungus to rejuvenate their union.

Disasters, it seems, have been my stock in trade. At least, I have never felt quite as comfortable as I do in the midst of a good, rending cataclysm. So many things fall into place, so much is settled for good or ill; I sometimes pray for more upheavals, if only to clear the air. But a disaster has its full share of negative values also. If you happen to be idly standing around, you find yourself clutched, scattered, or dragged away.

It's important to keep your wits about you at all times. Even so, it is often impossible to resist the emotional demands of weaker individuals. Thus it was that I found myself dragged away, down the spiral staircases of our St. Charles Avenue mansion and into the hot, sunny yard. Behind the house the spiky, gray-green plants were still bead-strung with drops from the afternoon's shower. The grass in the yard had been left to grow unchecked, and now the rough blades grasped up inside my labcoat, scraping unpleasantly on the bare skin of my legs below my Bermuda shorts.

There was a door set into the back of the house, a small door only five feet high; unlike the remainder of the mansion, the exterior of which was preserved as well as our budgets allowed, the door was a seedy tatter of another era. Its cream-colored paint was faded and dirty, tending now to peel and chip, littering the small flagstone walk with sad tear-flakes of pigment. I had on occasion asked Dr. Johnson what rested behind that anomalous door, but I had never succeeded in getting a straight answer. "It's the sickled grain room," he would reply. If I pushed him some more, he would go on in terrifying clichés about age and death and the fatal vanity of art.

"I know," I said, suddenly comprehending what ought to have been clear long before. "This is where you keep your pets, in whatever form they may take."

Dr. Johnson fiddled with the several locks. I watched the strong muscles of his back shifting beneath the coarse white duck of his labcoat. "They take only the grim forms of corruption," he said. I considered the uncountable ways he might have described the death of his pets, each way a monstrous perversion of literary style. But he had not chosen one of the more readily accessible clichés, after all. Perhaps he was recovering. I could only think that perhaps there was hope for my own romantic affliction.

He flung the door open. Standing in the bright glare of the yard, I could see nothing of the chamber beyond. Dr. Johnson entered, ducking his head; I followed, somewhat bored and resigned to offering my condolences. I stood beyond the threshold of the room for some seconds, waiting drowsily for my eyes to grow accustomed to the dimness. My nose rebelled immediately, however; mixed with the ancient, musty smell of a room long sealed away from the common business of a great house was the fetid odor of decay. The room itself was rotting, a spreading abscess devouring an entire corner of the mansion. But more than that, I sensed an overpowering presence of putrefying material, lately and voluntarily introduced by my friend.

Soon I could make out a series of roughhewn wooden tables set up in rows, each bearing small boxes of damp earth. In these I saw dozens of mushrooms, their thin stalks no longer able to support the weight of their huge, spreading caps. Dr. Johnson picked up one of the boxes and carried it into the daylight. At last, delivered in death into the full glare of the sun, their colors became evident. They were brilliantly hued underneath, though the stalks and the tops of the caps were a sick pinkish white.

"My pets!" said Dr. Johnson, in an odd whining voice.

"Remarkably phallic, aren't they?" I asked.

"Dead, all dead."

"That is the way of the world," I said. He stared at me for a few seconds. Then he roused himself, as though struck by some overpowering thought.

"Come, you must help me carry them all out." I shrugged. He was obviously deeply affected and, though he had spared few tears for my mollies, I felt bound to accede to his sudden wishes. Together we brought out the boxes of dead mushrooms, nearly a hundred containers in all. Dr. Johnson placed them against a low brick wall at the very back of the yard. A row of tall banana plants grew along the wall, and in the middle of the line a space had been left for some sort of arbor. The arbor itself had long since disappeared and its place been filled by a sapling crape myrtle purchased recently by my companion. Furiously he ripped the newly planted

And Us, Too, I Guess

tree from the ground, casting it carelessly over his shoulder. I ignored his frenzy. Then he began to dig. He seemed to forget my presence, so intent was he; it was just as well, as I had little desire to aid his foolishness. Hours later he had completed his task—a deep grave, lined with flagstones torn from the walk and driveway. His mushrooms (*fungi,* he insisted on calling them. They were fungi, not mushrooms) were safely buried beneath a towering cairn of stones and old wooden milk crates.

Days passed, and Dr. Johnson's grief did not abate. I mentioned once, casually, while bringing him a tray of broth and junket, that life must go on. He did not take the hint. I suggested he get another sort of pet. He only growled senselessly. He did not appear to want to work at all until he saw, quite by accident, a newscast in which a botanist somewhere in the great outback of North America described the coincidental demise of his own fungi. Then, later, came Dr. Waters' brilliant thesis. I remember the look on my colleague's face when he read that. He jumped out of bed, wearing the quaint hospital-style labcoat I had fashioned for him (cut out in the back), and ran to our typewriter. He wrote a letter of commiseration to the Iowa botanist, and a letter of admiration to Waters.

"I'm all right, now," he said to me afterward. "It's okay. As long as it's part of some cosmic something-or-other, I don't mind. In fact, I'm proud. Maybe the government will reimburse me."

How easily his fungi were forgotten; how grateful I was for the divine intervention. Now at last we had our goal and our first true data, all at once. We accepted as a given Dr. Waters' curious hypothesis. Perhaps every day a different species of animal or plant would leave this God-favored world for good and all; what an exciting prospect to research! It made little difference to us, as callous, disinterested members of the scientific community, what those species might be. But we had to know *how often* the phenomenon occurred. Such is the nature of science: what can be measured, what can be classified, named, catalogued, filed, documented, that was all that concerned us. How often did an entire species croak? We spent many sleepless nights debating, not on the length of the period (we agreed that it *must* be once *per diem*), but on the best method of proving it.

While we tackled the riddle from a purely technical, reasoned, dispassionate angle, the popular media began its hateful commercialism. Each day the Cleveland *States-Item* printed a little box on the front page, much as at Christmas a record of "shopping days left" is kept. The box was outlined with a heavy black border, and centered within, in small type, was the name of the species that, biologists had decided, had gone extinct the previous day, with a mawkish photo of it. It's hard to jerk a tear with a picture of a scarce Australian peat moss; but I'll never forget the day the kaji lemur passed away. Those huge, pleading eyes turned my stomach.

This went on for a while; most days the box was completely empty, meaning that the scientists had been unable to identify which of the innumerable species no longer was. Less frequently, there was some plant or animal I'd never heard of gracing the newspaper's lower left corner. I complained to Dr. Johnson, wishing that we could end the sentimental exploitation of our disaster. He scowled at me. "You're as bad as they are!" he said angrily. "What about the silkworm? What about the inkwell beetle? What about the diamondwort?" I could only shrug my shoulders and smile in embarrassment.

Through a quirk of the city's public transportation system, Paul arrived at work nearly fifteen minutes earlier than usual.

And Us, Too, I Guess

It was late September; already the mornings were retaining some of the night's icy chill. It would not be long before Paul would need a stronger incentive to face the winter cold. Still, the autumn sharpness excited him. The slight dash of cool air, the deeper blue of the sky, even the fresh rustling of the fading leaves revived him, made him realize that his narrow world could still be beautiful. But that annual discovery was too ephemeral; it never lived beyond the second snowfall, when the first already lay crushed and filthy.

Paul waited in the long line by the time clocks. He stood behind an older woman who was dressed in faded, torn coveralls. The woman carried a copy of the morning paper folded under her arm, her lunch pail in the other hand. Bored, waiting for the slow line to creep by the clock, Paul tried to read the bits of articles revealed by the woman's heavy arm. He saw the bottom part of the first page, the news index and the weather forecast. Beside that, half concealed by a fold of the woman's knit pullover, was the day's black box. Paul could see that it was not empty; another something had died off, the day before, perhaps. If the scientists had been able to decide what had gone extinct, it must have been a fairly common species.

Paul hoped that it was good and dramatic. He felt a little guilty as he stood in the line, straining to see what the paper said. In years gone by he had always turned to the obituary section with a thrilling, eager feeling: who knew what might be there? A beautiful movie star cut down in the prime of her career, an athlete tragically killed in a freak accident, a leader murdered, leaving a nation directionless—something to make the day special, something to talk about. "Did you hear? Korpaniev died. In his garage. They found him in the car with the motor running. Maybe suicide."

That was the way it used to be. Now Paul looked first at the little black box. Most mornings it was empty; the experts had not been able to determine just what had gone extinct the day before. Sometimes the box named a flower or a bug; that didn't mean that they had necessarily died within the previous twenty-four hours, of course. It was merely that the scientists had finally noticed their sudden absence. Day after day Paul hoped for something impressive; he was usually disappointed and had to turn to the obits, where celebrities still passed away in the old proportions.

More and more articles appeared in the paper, each taking some shrill position on the question of Dr. Bertram Waters' theory. Of course, most conservative biologists would not believe the matter really existed. There was no concrete proof, other than the ragged list of suddenly extinguished species. But that was not necessary-and-sufficient evidence that Waters was right. There could be no such evidence; the whole situation was too theological for serious scientists to argue. But, if Waters *happened* to be correct, then the entire rational basis of natural science meant nothing any longer anyway. Paul was content to skim a small portion of the debates and wait anxiously for something *big* to go: bears. What if every bear in the world died? Wouldn't *that* cause a fight?

One article a few days before had argued that the situation was a great deal more serious than anyone had yet imagined. Surely people like Paul and Linda could not be concerned over the extinction of *Cantepus nepifer,* a microscopic animal that lived in bogs and ponds and such. But, the author of the article continued, the *dirans* flatworm, which fed almost exclusively on the *nepifer,* would be in very bad shape. Perhaps the flatworm, too, would be driven to extinction; deprived of its natural food, it would die off before its natural turn.

The idea intrigued Paul. He had never before realized how interdependent things were. He did not get concerned, however; no, greater scientists than even the author of the article argued that introducing such concepts as a creature's "natural turn" automatically prejudiced the case by making the argument irresponsibly subjective. There was no way to debate the question without resort to scientifically untenable premises. Nevertheless the controversy raged, and the newspapers and magazines cheerfully served as a forum. And they continued to list the forever-gone animals and plants, one by one.

Paul adopted a patient, noncommittal attitude. More accurately, he didn't especially care and, like the majority of people with whom he discussed the situation, didn't particularly believe any of it. It was just another wild scientific theory, like the existence of life on other planets, or proof of Noah's Flood in the streaky strata of the Grand Canyon. The scientists were having fun fighting it out, and everyone was getting a scrap of entertainment, but the matter itself would probably be forgotten in a few weeks.

The line shuffled ahead. Paul leaned against a bulletin board, empty except for a single poster. The notice showed a decapitated body searching for its head, which rested far away, eyes x-ed out, as the bottom dot of an exclamation point that emphasized the words "Carelessness Costs!" "It don't make any difference," thought Paul as he examined the poster wearily. "My mollies led good molly lives. They were as careful as they could be. They honored their mothers and their fathers. It never did *them* any good." The line moved again. Paul arranged the spare thumbtacks on the board into a large *F*.

"Could I read your paper for a minute?" he said to the woman ahead of him in the line.

She turned around and regarded him blankly for a moment. "What?" she said.

"Could I see your paper?" The woman blinked, then

handed the newspaper to him. He nodded his thanks, unfolded the paper, and sought out the black box. The small type inside said *Norassis scotti*. There was a line drawing of a weirdly shaped tubular thing, with regular segments and large nuclear structures. Paul could see that it was some strange microscopic living thing, but whether it was an animal or plant he could not tell. He frowned and folded the newspaper. As an afterthought he reopened it and turned to the sports pages, to check the major league pennant playoffs. There was no good news there, either, and he returned the paper to the woman.

The day went by slowly. Paul worked on an assembly line during the morning, tightening the same six bolts on voltmeter chassis until lunchtime. In the afternoon he typed out Quality Control tags with lists of the subassemblers' code numbers. Then he went home. As soon as he stepped into the sunlight he forgot all the petty annoyances of the day. His job wasn't serious enough to make him rehearse his irritation after working hours. He showed up at the factory in the morning and stayed long enough to earn his paycheck; beyond that, the job had no existence.

He was glad to get home, nevertheless. He was tired, and he just wanted to watch the news and eat supper. He said hello to Linda (who failed to answer) and went straight into the bedroom. He lay down and switched on the television. The international and national news rarely interested him; the local news had relevance only slightly more often. But after the major items, and just before the sports and the weather report, the news program presented a summary of the day's activity among the scientists.

Linda came into the room. "Can't you hear me? I've called you three times now. If you want to eat, come on. I'm not going to serve you in here."

And Us, Too, I Guess

Paul looked up at her. She was his wife; she was even now carrying their first child, due to be born around the end of December. He knew it was foolish to be sentimental now, after so much bad feeling had grown up between them. Even the baby was a sore spot in their relationship; Linda never missed an opportunity to blame the unwanted pregnancy on his selfish appetites. She was probably frightened and unhappy; he certainly hadn't been doing anything to ease her anxiety. "Sit down for a while," he said. "Watch the news with me."

"The food's getting cold," she said. "I'm going to eat now. Bring the set out with you if you don't want to miss your program."

Paul pulled the television's cord from the wall and followed his wife into the kitchen. He put the set on the table and plugged it in. "We never watch anything together any more," he said, noticing that it was spaghetti for supper.

"Maybe that has something to do with the differences in our tastes. Maybe we're not as compatible as we used to be. Maybe *one* of us is growing and maturing, and the other is content to let his mind rot."

"Have you been paying any attention to how all these animals and things have been dying?" he asked.

Linda paused in her eating to stare at him. "No," she said, "I haven't. I have other things to do."

"It's just that somebody said today how all these tiny dead bugs and plants may hurt us, eventually. I mean, with them gone, the other animals have less to eat."

She gave him a scornful look. "Listen who has the big heart all of a sudden. He can't spare a minute for his own wife's pains, but he's worried sick about a lousy bug. Look, *we* won't have any trouble, and that's all that counts. As long as the A & P doesn't go out of business, we'll be all right."

"Never mind." Paul gave up his conciliatory effort. After all, he had made a decent try; the next move was up to Linda. He ate his supper resentfully and watched the news commentator, who was remarking on the potential danger caused by the sudden gaps appearing in the ecological food chains.

"What few people beside the scientific researchers can grasp," said the newsman, "is the idea that something as negligible as the pond scum in your backyard may be indirectly important to the well-being of your entire family. Though the individual plants that make up the algae layer are so tiny that they're invisible to the naked eye, they play an important role in the natural scheme of things. Besides serving as food for various larger creatures, they serve a critical function by aerating the water, supplying oxygen to the fish. One species of fresh-water algae became extinct over three weeks ago, and as a result the entire population of fishes in several lakes in Colorado was nearly wiped out. Fortunately, an alternate species of algae was artificially introduced by a local high school biology class.

"In the random pattern of Dr. Waters' theory, we cannot be sure what particular species of plant or animal will be next. Perhaps one day soon every shoot of *Oryza sativa,* or common rice, will die. It is not difficult to imagine what effect that will have on the nearly two billion people who depend on rice as their daily nourishment. That's certainly food for thought. This is Gil Monahan, Channel Ten News, New York."

"That's what I call yellow journalism," said Linda.

"Why?"

"Because he can't even prove what he's talking about, and the first thing he tries to do is scare the audience. Sure, it would be awful if all the rice in the world died overnight. But what are the odds of that happening?"

And Us, Too, I Guess

Paul got up and scraped the rest of his spaghetti into the garbage. "Yeah, you're right. But that doesn't mean it's wrong to be prepared."

"And maybe an airplane will fall out of the sky and smash you on your way to work tomorrow. Is that going to keep you home?"

Paul grimaced as he unplugged the television and carried it back to the bedroom. "Maybe it will," he said.

Above and beyond all considerations of mere change and transmutation, the pure panic of a disaster is fun to watch. I could see the symptoms already—my experience in these matters stood me in good stead—and I could hardly contain my excitement. I could tell no one, least of all Dr. Johnson, what I knew and what I could so easily foresee. My very good friend would himself provide many evenings' entertainment as I observed his placid frame of mind begin to fray around its selvaged border. His screams and hysterical pronouncements of doom were the sweetest music to me, for I understood that if such an unruffable sort as Dr. Johnson could be reduced to frenzy, the common crowd would soon break loose altogether.

I forgot one detail. The great masses were not as educated as my companion, and were for the most part totally ignorant of the implications of our disaster. Like those poor souls who lived on the very slopes of Vesuvius, they did not comprehend the proximity of death. And, like the survivors of that ancient Pompeiian spectacle who relocated themselves afterward on those same slopes, I don't suppose the masses especially cared. Human beings have carried within themselves the notion of their own superiority so long that it's very difficult for us to imagine a world without people. If a group or a city or even a nation is wiped out, other cities and nations remain to merely cluck tongues. I had no slightest desire to spell out the imminent doom; I wanted only to be around when the idea dawned on them all.

"We should stock up," said Dr. Johnson one morning. "We ought to get a large vehicle and raid a supermarket. Canned goods. We could live out our lives on canned goods if we had to, couldn't we? Meat, especially. What if all the cattle go? No more meat. Cases and cases of ravioli, that's what we need."

"And all the wheat?" I asked. "What if wheat goes tomorrow? Crackers will soon be very scarce. Of course, you can buy those tinned, I suppose, but that soon gets expensive. Particularly if you're thinking about forty years' worth of rations."

"Forget that," said Dr. Johnson irritably. "Never mind wheat. If wheat goes, we can get used to cornmeal products. Or rye bread. Rye toast with fresh butter and blackberry jam is one of the grandest things in the world. Surely the laws of chance prohibit the extinction of wheat, corn, and rye within a single lifetime."

"Then stop worrying about the cattle. There's always pork and lamb."

"You're insane!" he cried, and I only laughed gently. "What sort of ivory tower do you live in? Don't you see what's happening? Don't you *care?*"

Of course I saw. And no, I didn't care. Out with the old, in with the new! Great bloody holes were being ripped in the food chains that Mother Nature had so patiently devised over countless millennia. How would the world react? What would devour what? There are always certain special moments in one's life, like the day I awoke to learn that FDR had died. How stunning! What would happen next? How would the

And Us, Too, I Guess

powers realign themselves? Now I felt that precise emotion—what would happen next? How would nature realign things? Would the blue-point oyster find something else to live on, or choose a species-specific suicide by its overspecialized diet? And all Dr. Johnson (and the rest of the scientific community, for the most part) could think of was his own future.

I did not worry about myself. I knew that I could eat just about anything.

The public, which for so many weeks had ignored the increasingly strident warnings of Dr. Waters and his colleagues (us), now began to panic. They had been blind to the problem for so long that now, when they chose to see, the situation was far graver than their meager hope could battle. They reacted in typically bestial fashion. First, religion. Never before had so many prayers wafted heavenward, so much incense or whatever devoteeward, so many anguished moans helpless priestward. None of that worked, and I had little sympathy. In the meantime, with Dr. Johnson's weak-kneed aid, I made a killing by corralling the canned-sardine market in Cleveland's Irish Channel. I convinced several local store managers that the seas were dying, the algae had become extinct, the kelp and the seaweed, and that soon every fish in the ocean would be floating belly up to God. I sold cases and cases of hoarded sardines for remarkable profits, which I used to buy up all the pimentos in town. This proved to be a mistake. I digress.

Anyway, after religion the populace turned to politics, recapitulating the discoveries of universal folly they had all made as adolescents. Countries were urged to war to feed their citizens, all busily envisioning themselves starving on the morrow. No one had yet been beset by these hardships, of course; but Dr. Waters' prose was so persuasive that millions of people developed the most delicious sense of verging destruction. Any minute now, any minute and we'll have *nothing to eat.* I loved it.

Dr. Johnson went berserk. Having neither religion nor politics to turn to, having only the cold embrace of science, he imagined himself abandoned in the cosmos. He smashed every little bottle of chemicals we had; their contents drifted powdery to the floor, combining in useless mixtures which my friend tried to ignite. No success there. Then he thrust his bare arm into a cage of gerbils, bidding the timid beasts to gnaw his flesh. They would not. In an ecstasy of impotent terror he leaped headlong into a half-completed glassware sculpture, only to emerge with cuts over one eye and charming glitters of jeweled glass in his hair and beard.

As he knelt amid the silicate ruin, I touched his shoulder. "Have you had quite enough?" I asked.

"I will not see," he said, sobbing.

"Splinters in your eyes? Shards of glass tubing, unpolished by any Bunsen's flame, stabbing into the soft blueness of your irises?"

He only shook his head. I laughed quietly. Dr. Johnson was finally, completely broken. He had had enough, and I did not wish to cause him any further torture. I helped him rise, brushed off his wrinkled labcoat, ran a brotherly hand through his tangled hair to collect what bloody spikes of crystal I could, and urged him upstairs to bed. As we progressed slowly up that felted spiral, I wished that someone could do the same for the whole race of man. That was sadly impossible. I was needed here.

Dr. Johnson fell asleep quickly, thanks partly to the drug I had mixed into his milk and Bosco. I left him and returned downstairs, wondering if any more of our abandoned experimental animals had gone extinct since last I checked. On an impulse I threw open all the cages and set them free; hamsters and monkeys and others scampered or limped to the exit. I flung out the double shuttered doors; the animals trooped past, obviously in some bewilderment. I threw handfuls of lettuce and wood chips onto the gravel walk outside, and they soon got the idea. The next morning I saw only a single serpent, twined in the iron lace that fringed the pillars supporting the upstairs balcony.

Soon Dr. Johnson regained his mental balance. I read to him of other great catastrophes in the world's youth, from the Bible and various works of science fiction. He seemed greatly cheered by these recitals and began at last to ask me questions of our current situation, as though I had any more answers than he. I lied to him as best I could, and he improved steadily; soon, about the middle of November, he was well enough to accept my suggestion that we go on some sort of vacation. Even the idea of a fishing trip did not frighten him (it was the thought of poor slaughtered beasts that had driven him wacky, I later learned); he was very eager to go out into the world and get his limit while both he and the fish still existed. I nodded sagely. Everything was all right.

On the fifth of November, the sugar maples died.

It was the first really remarkable species to become extinct. It was very definitely the big thing that Paul had been waiting for. But when he saw the black box in the paper that evening, his reaction was rather one of anger, as though the power that caused the event had somehow rudely imposed on him.

"Did you see this?" he asked Linda, holding the newspaper out for her to read.

"What now? Something else die off?"

"Yeah, maple trees."

"That's too bad," she said. She didn't really look very concerned; she rested on the bed, spending the final five weeks of her gravidity conserving her energy. "Is that where we get syrup and stuff?"

"I guess so."

"Oh, well, as long as we still have sugarcane, never mind."

Paul tossed the paper onto the bed. "That's not the point," he said irritably. "This thing's turning into a pretty lousy inconvenience. It's got to be the air. Remember when everybody was saying the bad winters were on account of the Russians or the strontium 90 or something? Nobody ever talks about that anymore. I'll bet there was more truth in it than the government ever admitted. I'll bet this whole thing's our punishment for pollution."

Linda switched off the television impatiently. She had watched six hours of daytime game shows, and now the situation-comedy reruns were too much for her. "That's silly," she said. "What are the maple trees being punished for?"

"They always say that God moves in mysterious ways."

"God? Since when God? And those aren't *mysterious* ways you're talking about. They're childish and stupid."

"I don't know about anything else. I can't explain it. Sometimes it scares me."

"I still don't believe it's happening," said Linda, turning heavily on her side. "I haven't seen anything that's convinced me; I think a lot of supposedly smart people are getting hysterical over nothing."

Paul felt himself being led into the same argument they had had every day for nearly four months. "What more proof do you *want?* For crying out loud, every lousy sugar maple tree in the world just died, all together in one day, and you say nothing strange is happening."

Linda gave him a forced smile, broad and cold and mocking. "How do *I* know every maple tree in the world is dead?

And Us, Too, I Guess

Whose word am I taking? How do *they* know? How can you be sure there isn't one left, far away—in Pakistan, maybe?"

Paul sat on the edge of the bed. He reached across his wife's body to turn on the television again. When the picture came on, he changed the station, searching for the early-evening news. An ominous scene stopped his hand: a shaky film, shot with a hand-held camera while running down some nameless street, showed huge boiling clouds of smoke rising behind a row of stores. The windows of the shops were all smashed. Broken bottles and crates, overturned shopping carts, automobiles abandoned where they had smashed into walls or telephone poles, and merchandise, looted and thrown away as useless, littered the sidewalk. A figure farther down the street ran into view. The cameraman stopped, tried to focus on the other person, who threw something and ran. The scene jumped wildly, then settled down with the camera staring fixedly at the sky. The picture went black, and almost immediately a newscaster appeared to gloss the events.

"See," said Paul, "*somebody's* taking this awful serious. That's what it's been like out there. That's why I want to get out of the city so bad. People are starting to panic. If you got outside at all, you'd see it, too; but you just want to sulk in the apartment. You're not going to be able to save your skin like that. Not next month, when there isn't anything left to buy at the A & P."

"That film wasn't from the city," she said, her voice sounding frightened for the first time.

"No," said Paul, "I think that was supposed to be some little New England town. But it'll happen here, sooner or later. The city sort of insulates you against things. You get the idea that anything you want will be around somewhere, nearby. It's all an illusion. Everything we need has to be trucked in. We're more dependent on the outside world than anybody on earth. If food gets scarce, you can bet there won't be any happy farmers driving their own share over the bridge to feed us. It's happening already out in the country. The small-town stores are being emptied by hoarders."

"Paul," said Linda. He looked at her, but she was staring straight ahead. He hoped that she'd cry but knew that she wouldn't.

"What?"

"We can't go. The baby."

"I think that's a pretty good reason to get out while we can. We've got to find a place to hole up and wait for people to come to their senses."

"That won't work, Paul. It's people doing just that who are making the situation worse."

"So? Two more won't make any difference."

She turned to look at him. "Paul, I don't like this," she whispered.

"Me neither," he said, taking her hand and rubbing it. He was shocked to find her palm hot and clammy with sweat. "I'm supposed to be the protector and all that stuff. Just let me figure it out and we'll be okay. The three or four or five of us." He breathed heavily, then laughed when he saw her sudden smile.

"Just three," she said. "Don't overwork me."

The condition of life was degenerating. The frequent speeches by the scientists, far from making things clear, served only to confuse the already volatile situation. It was commonly accepted that Dr. Waters' warning was true, that certain species of animals and plants were spontaneously dying out. There seemed to be no pathological reason behind the situation, and no one, neither technologist nor clergyman, cared to offer an explanation. People were far too concerned with the effects to care about the reasons.

And Us, Too, I Guess

Paul doubted whether those effects were serious enough to justify the rioting and the looting, which were becoming more frequent every day. Sure, the order of things had been shaken up; important niches in the ecology had been suddenly left vacant. But the cumulative threat to mankind couldn't be very large, nor could whatever danger threatened become real in the near future. In the meantime, the scientific community had plenty of time to avert a general tragedy.

So Paul thought, until the ninth of December, the morning all the dogs were dead. On the way to the subway he saw one of the neighborhood mongrels lying on the sidewalk, its head and front legs falling over the curb. Paul felt a faint distaste, and hoped that someone would remove the dog's corpse before he came home. Less than thirty yards away was another dead dog, a German shepherd that belonged to an old Hispanic lady on the block. It always sat in the open window of the woman's apartment, staring at Paul as he walked by. Now it hung over the windowsill, its tongue swollen and protruding, its eyes opened sightlessly to the ground. A few flies hovered and settled on its muzzle. Paul suffered a touch of disgust, then a quick shock of fear. *The dogs!* Even the most stubborn of Waters' opponents would have a moment's alarm now.

Vindication was a poor trade for what the extinction of *Canis familiaris* would do to the teetering popular mind. Unable to understand what was happening, people everywhere were returning to primal instincts. There was no definite way to answer the challenge, though; no one could say just where the danger might arise. It was this helplessness, this failure of logic to advise one on how best to prepare, that destroyed man's thin shell of culture.

The Jennings Manufacturing Corporation was closed when Paul arrived. There were no signs, no explanations; large steel gates were drawn over the doors and locked with heavy chains. Workmen were busily bricking up the windows on the ground floor.

Paul went up to one of the men. "They're not even going to let me go in and clean out my locker?" he said.

The workman didn't turn around. "Nope," he said. "You'll have to wait until things settle down a little."

"Old Man Jennings must be figuring on a pretty long wait."

"Don't you?"

"I just wanted the instant coffee I left inside. You got a dog?"

"Yeah. Why?"

"Was he all right when you left home this morning?"

"I guess so," said the workman, putting down his trowel to gaze curiously at Paul. "I don't know; I didn't see him. Why?"

"He's dead." Paul shoved his hands deep into the pockets of his jacket and started walking back to the subway.

The bricklayer called after him. "Dogs, today? For God's sake, why *dogs?*" Paul shook his head and kept walking. Sooner or later the world was going to be in awful bad trouble. People needed to keep their emotions out of it. There had to be a sensible way to live in spite of the problem. Paul had seen the situation develop long before most of the rest; it was his long exposure and his uncertainty that held him from running into the street, screaming. Linda, who had tried to ignore the hints of calamity as long as possible, had at last admitted her blindness. Suddenly forced to deal with a nightmare of doubts, she had thrown herself completely into Paul's care, hoping that he knew better what to do. It had been a bitter trial for her; she had always prided herself on her independence and her reasonable outlook. Now it seemed that reason had little survival value. Confronted with a completely illogical environment, she preferred to have someone else assume the responsibilities. She hid from herself the fact that Paul was no better equipped to take over those functions.

"Hey, Linda?" he called, when he got home.

"Paul? Why are you back so soon?"

He went into the bedroom, where Linda was already awake, watching an early women's panel show. "Jennings closed down the plant. I guess he didn't want the riffraff getting in and tearing up his pile of soldering irons. So it looks like I'm out of a job for a while."

"They were talking about how bad things are getting in Asia. This guy was saying that the people are falling back into tribes and all sorts of stuff. He says he can see it happening everywhere, even here. Everybody's predicting the end of the world, but I look out the window and I can't see anything different."

"You look out now, you'll see a lot of dead dogs."

"Huh? Dogs? What happened?"

"All the dogs died," said Paul. "Like the trees and bugs and germs. Just that now the thing is a lot more obvious. If you think people were rattled before, just wait."

Linda hadn't really accepted the news. "Is it some kind of disease? Why haven't they come up with a shot or a pill or something?"

"And give it to every living thing in the world? No, it looks like all we can do is watch. This isn't something you can beat with a stick."

"Paul, would you lie here with me for a while?"

He was glad to rest. He was very frightened; he knew that there must be a safe course to follow, some way to protect his family and himself. But he didn't know how to find out about it.

"It has come to the point where I must believe my own

truisms," said Dr. Johnson sadly. I had not been paying close attention, and had to ask him to explain. The sun was warm, though the mid-December air was chilly. I sat in our small boat, drowsing with the gently rocking motion, and gratefully deferred to my companion all intellectual activity.

"We're scraping the bottom of the barrel," he said, and I thrilled to the return of the old trite him. "We're really in a pickle now, and there's nothing for it but to muddle through. What guideposts have we? Only those we build ourselves, out of desperation and ignorance. Science, science, why have you forsaken us?"

"That is not strictly so," I said sleepily. "Science has not deserted us at all. Merely transcended. We fail to understand. Our fault, entirely. We're looking for answers in the same dried-up old wells."

"Perhaps," said Dr. Johnson in his customary thoughtful way, "and perhaps not." He was such a comical sight, sitting in the stern of our little rowboat, dressed in his wrinkled white labcoat and a beat-up old hat stuck with badly made fishing flies. He held his fishing pole stiffly, staring constantly at the point where the line disappeared beneath the slow ripples. I had warned him several times to relax, or suffer cramped muscles later, but he would not listen. He was determined to catch more fish than I, and to do it by concentration. I had not even brought my fishing equipment, to make it easier for him.

"There's a chance all these fish will be extinct tomorrow, so you'd better do as well as possible this afternoon," I said jokingly. He nodded grimly. Only two days before we set out into the bayou area surrounding Cleveland, a popular local species of bait worm had died out, and the prices on everything else had immediately skyrocketed. Such is my luck.

The great muddy river, carrying with it the rich effluvia of

And Us, Too, I Guess

its mighty journey, rolled at last near its goal; the bayou country, where the river's fresh water mingled with the salty fingers of the sea, was an eerie, lovely, hazardous place. Immense oak trees, all shaggy with Spanish moss still, though their own leaves had long since died, marked the scattered scraps of solid ground. The maple trees, each dead now, looked forlorn among the verdant splendors we had found not thirty miles from our laboratory on St. Charles Avenue. Cleveland itself was being slowly destroyed as its inhabitants grew more violently frustrated. But here, in the lonely beauty of the virgin marshlands, I could yet pretend that all was well, that some benevolent hand had created our earth as a bountiful park for man's enjoyment.

"We may never have to work again," said Dr. Johnson, reeling in his line to see how much sourdough he had left. He never used his flies; they were mostly just for atmosphere. "I don't see any reason to expect this perplexing situation—"

"Disaster," I said cheerfully.

"Yes, disaster, you're right. Anyway, I see no cause to believe that it will end suddenly."

"Other than the fact that it began suddenly as well."

Dr. Johnson grasped his fishing pole awkwardly, up at arm's length, while he swung the line pendulum-fashion. Finally, with an inept jerk of the wrist, he loosed the weighted string into the water. He had not accurately coordinated his jerk with the line's arc, and the hook and sinker splashed into the green stuff that lapped against the side of the boat. Dr. Johnson smiled happily. "You're wrong again," he said. "There's no way of telling when these species began biting the dust. Who knows? Perhaps this is the explanation for the rather abrupt demise of the dinosaurs. It wouldn't have taken much to alter fatally their unstable environment. Just a minor food plant becoming extinct overnight. That would decimate the herbivores; the carnivores would soon follow in the familiar domino theory."

"You've got it all figured out, haven't you?" I said. He only nodded, a simpleminded grin on his face.

"I think I may go back to college and delve into German literature," he said later, while he let the various aquatic creatures feast on his sourdough.

"Which college?" I asked skeptically, aware that institutions were tumbling by the wayside all over the world.

"I don't know. I don't suppose the more established universities are having as much difficulty as the less exclusive."

"Sure they are," I said. "They're targets. Besides, you're only seeking sanctuary. You've lost the real drive, the sincere passion for knowledge to which you devoted yourself in your youth."

"Times have changed." He re-doughed his hook; I could only make scornful sounds, which he ignored.

He had some points, of course. Things were different now, and no amount of prayer could make them back into what they had been. Football, for instance, had had to make great allowances for the insanity of the fans. The crowds shrank from week to week, until only a dozen or so spectators turned out for the eleventh game of the season, between the Browns and the Rams. After that, the remainder of the schedule was suspended. It was a shame, too, because at that time it looked like the Browns had great Super Bowl chances.

The Detroit Lions had begun the season with a publicity stunt. Readers of the one still operating newspaper in the Motor City were asked to suggest an alternate nickname for the team, in the event of the current calamity befalling the species *Panthera leo*. The paper was stunned when not a single entry was submitted. The editor in charge of the contest came up with a phony winner—the Detroit Autoworkers,

And Us, Too, I Guess

though it proved to be a shortsighted choice; when things deteriorated further, there were definitely fewer autoworkers around than lions. The Yale Bulldogs, however, stuck with more traditions than they could handle, stuck also with their nickname. The original bulldog, stuffed in a trophy case in the school's gymnasium, took on a new and sadder significance.

As darkness began to fall, we headed the little skiff back to the island campsite. Dr. Johnson had caught no fish, but had not lost his abounding good humor. He was still trying to save the last bit of sourdough from his rusty hook, in a mistaken attempt at economy. The light was falling, and I watched his clumsy maneuvers with some dismay.

"Perhaps it's well that we're going back to Cleveland tomorrow afternoon," I said, making an unkind reference to his total failure as a woodsman.

"Why do you say that?" he asked innocently, looking up from his sticky labors.

"Because we're too isolated here. We have no idea of what's going on in the world. We may have some terrifying surprises waiting for us."

"You're an alarmist."

Yes, but not the way he meant. "It's situations like this," I said, "that so often breed subsidiary plagues and social unrest."

"You may have a point. It would be extremely unfortunate if, say, rats were among the next species to disappear."

That was an odd thing for him to say. For five minutes we glided across the turgid water, and I held myself in check. Finally I couldn't stand it and asked him. "Why would it be so bad if the rats died?"

He grinned. He knew he had scored a point; I was still well ahead, though, because he still hadn't cleaned his hook. "It's not rats that are so bad," he said. "As far as your plagues are concerned, I mean. It's the plague-carrying fleas *on* the rats. If the rats were gone, the fleas would have to find other hosts. And that has always meant humans in the past. The great black plagues of history have generally coincided with efforts to reduce the rat population."

"Oh."

"Rats!"

"Yes," I said wearily, "I know. Let's hope they thrive."

"No," said Dr. Johnson, his voice strangely muffled, "that was an interjection. I stuck myself with this hook."

Another metaphysical point for me. I could barely see his outline against the now starry sky; one hand was raised to his mouth as he soothed the savaged thumb. He was a good friend, and I'll probably never meet his like again. Of all my co-workers, my co-strivers after *scientia*, I guess that Dr. Johnson most closely filled my image of the truly wise man that I had formed in my undisciplined schooldays. But it is always the *fittest* who survive, not, as popular thought has it, the strongest. Perhaps it was fate that kept me from bringing my own fishing equipment; perhaps I have earned some special favor of destiny, I know not. But I thank my lucky stars that it wasn't I fiddling with the sourdough in that boat.

When we pulled the little skiff up on the grass of our campsite, I noticed that Dr. Johnson was still sucking on his wounded thumb. "What's wrong?" I asked.

"It doesn't want to stop bleeding," he said.

"You must have stabbed it pretty deep."

"No, not so bad. It ought to have quit by now."

"Have you tried direct pressure?"

He sighed in the gloom. "I've been doing that for ten minutes."

I felt a tiny, cold glitter of something. Slowly the thought took shape. "You know what I think?" I said. "I think we've

And Us, Too, I Guess

hit the big time. It's possible that a couple of days ago the special little bacteria that live in our intestines died off. You know, the ones that produce most of the vitamin K our bodies use. You need that vitamin K because it's vitally important to the clotting of blood. Hospitals give newborn babies doses of vitamin K because newborns don't have colonies of that bacterium in their bowels. Now, if that little bacterium is extinct, we're going to have a lot of people with blood that won't stop bleeding. And then there's going to be a rush on vitamin K. And then there won't be enough, and people won't be able to get their hands on it, and then—"

"I think you're getting carried away. That's not very scientific at all, is it? I mean, you deduce all this from the bad cut on my thumb."

"I'm not deducing," I said testily. "I'm hoping."

"It's grotesque."

"And then there'll be riots, but the officials will be helpless, and more and more people will start hemorrhaging. We'll have a world of hemophiliacs! And before anybody can do anything about it, it'll be too late. We won't have to wait until all the food vanishes." I was very excited, but worried, too, because my hypothesis was built on rather thin evidence.

"Your hypothesis is pretty shaky," said Dr. Johnson, echoing my thoughts in that winsome manner of his.

I decided to perform a serious experiment. I felt it prudent to know the truth before I returned to Cleveland, so that I might be ready for the worst. That night, after Dr. Johnson and I had retired to our sleeping bags, I pretended to fall asleep quickly. Dr. Johnson had no difficulty dropping off, after the long, exciting day on the water. I crept from my zippered bag and moved soundlessly to his side. I made a careful incision on the inside of his arm with my scaling knife, about one half inch long and deep enough to start a copious flow of blood; I also could not avoid rousing him from his slumber.

"What are you doing?" he asked sleepily.

"Binding you with stout cords," I said, which is what I was doing at that point. I suppose I ought to have done that first; that's what experiments are for, to learn these things. I made a mental note.

He complained that the incision gave him some discomfort. I opened the first-aid kit and allowed him two aspirins, no water. Then I sat down to wait for results; the blood ran freely, never slowing down during a period of fifteen minutes. I tried to stanch the rivulet with a gauze pad, but that had no effect. By morning Dr. Johnson's heart had pumped enough of the viscid fluid to foul his sleeping bag beyond possible hope of cleansing. I said good-bye to my friend and went outside to wait for the boat to take me back to Cleveland.

It was very cold. The oil companies had stopped delivering fuel, and the day before the Morans' apartment building had burned its last. Paul and Linda lay in bed, bundled as warmly as they could manage, but still shivering and exhausted from a poor night's sleep.

"I ought to go out today," said Paul. "I could get us a stove that burned wood and stuff. And we'll need more food soon."

"Don't go, Paul. I'm sure the baby's due today. I just know it. You won't be able to find a doctor, and I don't want to be alone when it comes."

Paul threw back the pile of clothing and blankets angrily. "Oh, I don't know anymore," he said, getting up and pacing the floor. "I can't see that I'll be any use whether I'm here or gone."

"I need you, Paul," she said. "We need each other. We just don't have anybody else in the world anymore."

He looked at her, lying helpless beneath the ineffectual layers of material. Her face had become lined with worry; her hair, once her greatest pride in whatever shrill tint it wore, was matted and dull. The mythical glow of motherhood had somehow passed her by, but Paul didn't mind that. He saw her now in a way he had never imagined possible. The heavy weight of life in the newly hard times had crushed all the false, selfish values she had cherished. Without the neurotic need to create problems, she had become a saner, truer person. He hoped fervently that the same thing had happened to himself.

"You were right," he said flatly. "You were always right. We should have gotten out of the city when we had the chance. Now it's too late; we're stuck here."

"Only until the baby comes," she said. "Then we can leave. I know things will be better. There's no reason at all why we have to stay up north. If it's going to be this bad, we may as well go down where it's not so cold. We can even go to Mexico, maybe. And then we won't have trouble about food—we can just pick it off the trees." She smiled at him, and he felt very lonely.

"So what happens when the baby comes? That scares me out of my mind."

"You've been reading that book I gave you, haven't you? So don't worry. Mine isn't the first baby that's ever been born; just do what it says. Other husbands have delivered. Policemen do it all the time."

"What if something goes wrong?"

Linda forced another smile. "What's to go wrong?" she asked. Paul could think of several things without trying very hard, but he said nothing.

Paul stood by the window, praying that everything would turn out all right. Outside, the street seemed very hostile. The garbage had been accumulating for over a week, and as it spilled and blew across the sidewalks it gave the city a fearful, abandoned look. He thought that it was odd how closely the street's appearance matched his own inner landscape.

"How are your teeth today?" asked Linda.

Paul turned around and laughed. "You're about to have a kid right there by yourself, and you're worried about my teeth."

"If you're not in good shape, you won't be able to pull your weight," she said with a mock-serious expression.

"They're still bleeding a lot," said Paul. "They won't stop. I would have thought they'd stop bleeding a long time ago."

"You're not getting enough vitamins or something."

"I'm just tired of living off canned food. I'd love some good meat right now, but nobody around here's got any."

"I've been bleeding, too," said Linda in a small voice. "It started last night."

"I know. I guess it's natural."

"I never heard of anything like that. I just want it to stop. The mattress is soaked."

"Now *you're* the one who's worrying too much," said Paul.

"You know what I'd like?"

Paul sat by her on the edge of the bed. "No. What?"

Linda smiled. "I think it would be great if one morning we woke up and all the cockroaches in the world were dead. It could happen, couldn't it?"

"Sure," said Paul grimly. "But you know what everybody forgets in the middle of all his little problems? Maybe one morning the cockroaches will wake up and all the *people* will be dead. It could happen just as easy. I mean, if different animals and plants are going one after another, that probably means human beings will have a natural turn, too. From now on when we go to sleep at night, we'll never be sure if we'll wake up in the morning."

"I thought about that once, but I didn't want to mention it. Anyway, you *never* know if you'll wake up. You have to face that."

"There's a big difference," said Paul. "The idea of your own death is somewhere off in the hazy future. If you're our age, dying in your sleep won't be a serious probability for fifty years. But the extinction of everybody is different. I can't accept it calmly, but it's there, and I can't fight against it. We'll never know. It could happen tomorrow."

"No, tomorrow is a day for new babies," said Linda. "I don't want to talk about death anymore. We're going to have a baby soon. It's going to have to grow up in this falling-down world, but it'll learn the new tricks fast. Our baby won't have any trouble. Then, when we get old, he can take care of us; that's funny to think about. You have to look at it that way, too, Paul. It's not such an awful, hopeless situation. We've already made a lot of adjustments." She squeezed his hand, and he kissed her lightly. "We just have to make a few more, that's all," she whispered weakly, a first tear beginning to trail down her dry cheek.

"That's all," whispered Paul, watching the dark-red stain around her grow slowly larger.

Chains of the Sea

GARDNER R. DOZOIS

Gardner Dozois sold his first story in 1966, when he was seventeen; but then he entered the Army, serving in Europe as a military journalist, and four years went by before he appeared in print again as a science-fiction writer. Since then his stories have been published in many magazines and anthologies, he has edited an anthology himself (A Day in the Life, 1972), and he has begun work on a novel. Several of his short stories have been nominees for the Nebula award, and his long novelet "A Special Kind of Morning" was a runner-up for both the Hugo and the Nebula in 1972. Mr. Dozois makes his home in Philadelphia.

One day the aliens landed, just as everyone always said they would. They fell out of a guileless blue sky and into the middle of a clear, cold November day, four of them, four alien ships drifting down like the snow that had been threatening to fall all week. America was just shouldering its way into daylight as they made planetfall, so they landed there: one in the Delaware Valley about fifteen miles north of Philadelphia, one in Ohio, one in a desolate region of Colorado, and one—for whatever reason—in a cane field outside of Caracas, Venezuela. To those who actually saw them come down, the ships seemed to fall rather than to descend under any intelligent control: a black nailhead suddenly tacked to the sky, coming all at once from nowhere, with no transition, like a Fortean rock squeezed from a high-appearing point, hanging way up there and winking intolerably bright in the sunlight; and then gravity takes hold of it, visibly, and it begins to fall, far away and dream-slow at first, swelling larger, growing huge, unbelievably big, a mountain hurled at the earth, falling with terrifying speed, rolling in the air, tumbling end over end, overhead, coming down—and then it is sitting peacefully on the ground; it has not crashed, and although it didn't slow and it didn't stop, there it *is,* and not even a snowflake could have settled onto the frozen mud more lightly.

To those photo reconnaissance jets fortunate enough to be flying a routine pattern at thirty thousand feet over the

Eastern Seaboard when the aliens blinked into their airspace, to the automatic, radar-eyed, computer-reflexed facilities at USADCOM Spacetrack East, and to the United States Aerospace Defense Command HQ in Colorado Springs, although they didn't have convenient recon planes up for a double check—the picture was different. The high-speed cameras showed the landing as a *process:* as if the alien spaceships existed simultaneously everywhere along their path of descent, stretched down from the stratosphere and gradually sifting entirely to the ground, like confetti streamers thrown from a window, like slinkys going down a flight of stairs. In the films, the alien ships appeared to recede from the viewpoint of the reconnaissance planes, vanishing into perspective, and that was all right, but the ships also appeared to dwindle away into infinity from the viewpoint of Spacetrack East on the ground, and that definitely was not all right. The most constructive comment ever made on this phenomenon was that it was odd. It was also odd that the spaceships had not been detected approaching Earth by observation stations on the Moon, or by the orbiting satellites, and nobody ever figured that out, either.

From the first second of contact to touchdown, the invasion of Earth had taken less than ten minutes. At the end of that time, there were four big ships on the ground, shrouded in thick steam—*not* cooling off from the friction of their descent, as was first supposed; the steam was actually mist: everything had frozen solid in a fifty-foot circle around the ships, and the quick-ice was now melting as temperatures rose back above freezing—frantic messages were snarling up and down the continent-wide nervous system of USADCOM, and total atomic war was a hair's breadth away. While the humans scurried in confusion, the Artifical Intelligence (AI) created by MIT/Bell Labs linked itself into the network of high-speed, twentieth-generation computers placed at its disposal by a Red Alert Priority, evaluated data thoughtfully for a minute and a half, and then proceeded to get in touch with its opposite number in the Soviet. It had its own, independently evolved methods of doing this, and achieved contact almost instantaneously, although the Pentagon had not yet been able to reach the Kremlin—that didn't matter anyway; they were only human, and all the important talking was going on in another medium. AI "talked" to the Soviet system for another seven minutes, while eons of time clicked by on the electronic scale, and World War III was averted. Both Intelligences finally decided that they didn't understand what was going on, a conclusion the human governments of Earth wouldn't reach for hours, and would never admit at all.

The only flourish of action took place in the three-minute lag between the alien touchdown and the time AI assumed command of the defense network, and involved a panicked general at USADCOM HQ and a malfunction in the—never actually used—fail-safe system that enabled him to lob a small tactical nuclear device at the Colorado landing site. The device detonated at point-blank range, right against the side of the alien ship, but the fireball didn't appear. There didn't seem to be an explosion at all. Instead, the hull of the ship turned a blinding, incredibly hot white at the point of detonation, faded to blue-white, to a hellish red, to sullen tones of violet that flickered away down the spectrum. The same pattern of precessing colors chased themselves around the circumference of the ship until they reached the impact point again, and then the hull returned to its former dull black. The ship was unharmed. There had been no sound, not even a whisper. The tactical device had been a clean bomb, but instruments showed that no energy or radiation had been released at all.

After this, USADCOM became very thoughtful.

Tommy Nolan was already a half hour late to school, but he wasn't hurrying. He dawdled along the secondary road that led up the hill behind the old sawmill, and watched smoke go up in thick black lines from the chimneys of the houses below, straight and unwavering in the bright, clear morning, like brushstrokes against the sky. The roofs were made of cold gray and red tiles that winked sunlight at him all the way to the docks, where clouds of sea gulls bobbed and wheeled, dipped and rose, their cries coming faint and shrill to him across the miles of chimneys and roofs and aerials and wind-tossed treetops. There was a crescent sliver of ocean visible beyond the dock, like a slitted blue eye peering up over the edge of the world. Tommy kicked a rock, kicked it again, and then found a tin can which he kicked instead, clattering it along ahead of him. The wind snatched at the fur on his parka, *puff*, momentarily making the cries of the sea gulls very loud and distinct, and then carrying them away again, back over the roofs to the sea. He kicked the tin can over the edge of a bluff, and listened to it somersault invisibly away through the undergrowth. He was whistling tunelessly, and he had taken his gloves off and stuffed them in his parka pocket, although his mother had told him specifically not to, it was so cold for November. Tommy wondered briefly what the can must feel like, tumbling down through the thick ferns and weeds, finding a safe place to lodge under the dark, secret roots of the trees. He kept walking, skuff-skuffing gravel very loudly. When he was halfway up the slope, the buzz saw started up at the mill on the other side of the bluff. It moaned and shrilled metallically, whining up through the stillness of the morning to a piercing shriek that hurt his teeth, then sinking low, low, to a buzzing, grumbling roar, like an angry giant muttering in the back of his throat. *An animal,* Tommy thought, although he knew it was a saw. *Maybe it's a dinosaur.* He shivered deliciously. *A dinosaur!*

Tommy was being a puddle jumper this morning. That was why he was so late. There had been a light rain the night before, scattering puddles along the road, and Tommy had carefully jumped over every one between here and the house. It took a long time to do it right, but Tommy was being very conscientious. He imagined himself as a machine, a vehicle— a puddle jumper. No matter that he had legs instead of wheels, and arms and a head, that was just the kind of ship he was, with he himself sitting somewhere inside and driving the contraption, looking out through the eyes, working the pedals and gears and switches that made the ship go. He would drive himself up to a puddle, maneuver very carefully until he was in exactly the right position, backing and cutting his wheels and nosing in again, and then put the ship into jumping gear, stomp down on the accelerator, and let go of the brake switch. And away he'd go, like a stone from a catapult, *up,* the puddle flashing underneath, then *down,* with gravel jarring hard against his feet as the earth slapped up to meet him. Usually he cleared the puddle. He'd only splashed down in water once this morning, and he'd jumped puddles almost two feet across. A pause then to check his systems for amber damage lights. The board being all green, he'd put the ship in *travel* gear and drive along some more, slowly, scanning methodically for the next puddle. All this took considerable time, but it wasn't a thing you could skimp on—you had to do it right.

He thought occasionally, *Mom will be mad again,* but it lacked force and drifted away on the wind. Already breakfast this morning was something that had happened a million years ago—the old gas oven lighted for warmth and hissing comfortably to itself, the warm cereal swimming with lumps, the radio speaking coldly in the background about things he never bothered to listen to, the gray hard light pouring through the window onto the kitchen table.

Mom had been puffy-eyed and coughing. She had been watching television late and had fallen asleep on the couch again, her cloth coat thrown over her for a blanket, looking very old when Tommy came out to wake her before breakfast and to shut off the humming test pattern on the TV. Tommy's father had yelled at her again during breakfast, and Tommy had gone into the bathroom for a long time, washing his hands slowly and carefully until he heard his father leave for work. His mother pretended that she wasn't crying as she made his cereal and fixed him "coffee," thinned dramatically with half a cup of cold water and a ton of milk and sugar, "for the baby," although that was exactly the way she drank it herself. She had already turned the television back on, the moment her husband's footsteps died away, as if she couldn't stand to have it silent. It murmured unnoticed in the living room, working its way through an early children's show that even Tommy couldn't bear to watch. His mother said she kept it on to check the time so that Tommy wouldn't be late, but she never did that. Tommy always had to remind her when it was time to bundle him into his coat and leggings and rubber boots—when it was raining—for school. He could never get rubber boots on right by himself, although he tried very hard and seriously. He always got tangled up anyway.

He reached the top of the hill just as the buzz saw chuckled and sputtered to a stop, leaving a humming, vibrant silence behind it. Tommy realized that he had run out of puddles, and he changed himself instantly into a big, powerful land tank as they showed on the war news on television, that could run on caterpillar treads or wheels and had a hovercraft air cushion for the tough parts. Roaring, and revving his engine up and down, he turned off the gravel road into the thick stand of fir forest. He followed the footpath, tearing along terrifically on his caterpillar treads, knocking the trees down and crushing them into a road for him to roll on. That made him uneasy, though, because he loved trees. He told himself that the trees were only being bent down under his weight, and that they sprang back up again after he passed, but that didn't sound right. He stopped to figure it out. There was a quiet murmur in the forest, as if everything were breathing very calmly and rhythmically. Tommy felt as if he'd been swallowed by a huge, pleasant green creature, not because it wanted to eat him, but just to let him sit peacefully in its stomach for shelter. Even the second-growth saplings were taller than he was. Listening to the forest, Tommy felt an urge to go down into the deep woods and talk to the Thants, but then he'd never get to school at all. Wheels would get tangled in roots, he decided, and switched on the hovercraft cushion. He floated down the path, pushing the throttle down as far as it would go, because he was beginning to worry a little about what would happen to him if he was *too* late.

Switching to wheels, he bumped out of the woods and onto Highland Avenue. Traffic was heavy here; the road was full of big trucks and tractor trailers on the way down to Boston, on the way up to Portland. Tommy had to wait almost ten minutes before traffic had thinned out enough for him to dash across to the other side of the road. His mother had told him never to go to school this way, so this was the way he went every chance he got. Actually, his house was only a half mile away from the school, right down Walnut Street, but Tommy always went by an incredibly circuitous route. He didn't think of it that way—it took him by all his favorite places.

So he rolled along the road shoulder comfortably enough,

following the avenue. There were open meadows on this side of the road, full of wild wheat and scrub brush, and inhabited by families of Jeblings, who flitted back and forth between the road, which they shunned, and the woods on the far side of the meadow. Tommy called to them as he cruised by, but Jeblings are always shy, and today they seemed especially skittish. They were hard to see straight on, like all of the Other People, but he could catch glimpses of them out of the corner of his eyes: spindly, beanstalk bodies, big pumpkinheads, glowing slit eyes, absurdly long and tapering fingers. They were in constant motion—he could hear them thrashing through the brush, and their shrill, nervous giggling followed him for quite a while along the road. But they wouldn't come out, or even stop to talk to him, and he wondered what had stirred them up.

As he came in sight of the school, a flight of jet fighters went by overhead, very high and fast, leaving long white scars across the sky, the scream of their passage trailing several seconds behind them. They were followed by a formation of bigger planes, going somewhat slower. *Bombers?* Tommy thought, feeling excited and scared as he watched the big planes drone out of sight. Maybe this was going to be the War. His father was always talking about the War, and how it would be the end of everything—a proposition that Tommy found interesting, if not necessarily desirable. Maybe that was why the Jeblings were excited.

The bell marking the end of the day's first class rang at that moment, cutting Tommy like a whip, and frightening him far more than his thoughts of the War. *I'm really going to catch it,* Tommy thought, breaking into a run, too panicked to turn himself into anything other than a boy, or to notice the new formation of heavy bombers rumbling in from the northeast.

By the time he reached the school, classes had already

finished changing, and the new classes had been in progress almost five minutes. The corridors were bright and empty and echoing, like a fluorescently lighted tomb. Tommy tried to keep running once he was inside the building, but the clatter he raised was so horrendous and terrifying that he slowed to a walk again. It wasn't going to make any difference anyway, not anymore, not now. He was already in for it.

Everyone in his class turned to look at him as he came in, and the room became deadly quiet. Tommy stood in the doorway, horrified, wishing that he could crawl into the ground, or turn invisible, or run. But he could do nothing but stand there, flushing with shame, and watch everyone watch him. His classmates' faces were snide, malicious, sneering and expectant. His friends, Steve Edwards and Bobbie Williamson, were grinning nastily and slyly, making sure that the teacher couldn't see. Everyone knew that he was going to get it, and they were eager to watch, feeling self-righteous and, at the same time, being glad that it wasn't they who had been caught. Miss Fredricks, the teacher, watched him icily from the far end of the room, not saying a word. Tommy shut the door behind him, wincing at the tremendous noise it made. Miss Fredricks let him get all the way to his desk and allowed him to sit down—feeling a sudden surge of hope—before she braced him and made him stand up again.

"Tommy, you're late," she said coldly.

"Yes, ma'am."

"You are very late." She had the tardy sheet from the previous class on her desk, and she fussed with it as she talked, her fingers repeatedly flattening it out and wrinkling it again. She was a tall, stick-thin woman, in her forties, although it really wouldn't have made any difference if she'd been sixty, or twenty—all her juices had dried up years ago, and she had become ageless, changeless, and imperishable, like a mummy. She seemed not so much shriveled as baked in some odd oven of life into a hard, tough, leathery substance, like meat that is left out in the sun turns into jerky. Her skin was fine-grained, dry, and slightly yellowed, like parchment. Her breasts had sagged down to her waist, and they bulged just above the belt of her skirt, like strange growths or tumors. Her face was a smooth latex mask.

"You've been late for class twice this week," she said precisely, moving her mouth as little as possible. "And three times last week." She scribbled on a piece of paper and called him forward to take it. "I'm giving you another note for your mother, and I want her to sign it this time, and I want you to bring it back. Do you understand?" She stared directly at Tommy. Her eyes were tunnels opening through her head onto a desolate ocean of ice. "And if you're late again, or give me any more trouble, I'll make an appointment to send you down to see the school psychiatrist. And *he'll* take care of you. Now go back to your seat, and let's not have any more of your nonsense."

Tommy returned to his desk and sat numbly while the rest of the class rolled ponderously over him. He didn't hear a word of it and was barely aware of the giggling and whispered gibes of the children on either side of him. The note bulked incredibly heavy and awkward in his pocket; it felt hot, somehow. The only thing that called his attention away from the note, toward the end of the class, was his increasing awareness of the noise that had been growing louder and louder outside the windows. The Other People were moving. They were stirring all through the woods behind the school, they were surging restlessly back and forth, like a tide that has no place to go. That was not their usual behavior at all. Miss Fredricks and the other children didn't seem to hear anything unusual, but to Tommy it was clear enough to take his mind off even his present trouble, and he stared curiously out the window into the gritty, gray morning.

Something was happening. . . .

The first action taken by the human governments of Earth —as opposed to the actual government of Earth: AI and his counterpart Intelligences—was an attempt to hush up everything. The urge to conceal information from the public had become so ingrained and habitual as to constitute a tropism— it was as automatic and unavoidable as a yawn. It is a fact that the White House moved to hush up the alien landings before the administration had any idea that they were alien landings; in fact, before the administration had any clear conception at all of what it was that they were trying to hush up. Something spectacular and very unofficial had happened, so the instinctive reaction of government was to sit on it and prevent it from hatching in public. Forty years of media-centered turmoil had taught them that the people didn't need to know anything that wasn't definitely in the script. It is also a fact that the first official governmental representatives to reach any of the landing sites were concerned exclusively with squelching all publicity of the event, while the heavily armed military patrols dispatched to defend the country from possible alien invasion didn't arrive until later—up to three quarters of an hour later in one case—which defined the priorities of the administration pretty clearly. This was an election year, and the body would be tightly covered until they decided if it could be potentially embarrassing.

Keeping the lid down, however, proved to be difficult. The Delaware Valley landing had been witnessed by hundreds of thousands of people in Pennsylvania and New Jersey, as the Ohio landing had been observed by a majority of the citizens in the North Canton–Canton–Akron area. The first people to reach the alien ship—in fact, the first humans to reach any of the landing sites—were the crew of a roving television van from a big Philadelphia station who had been covering a lackluster monster rally for the minority candidate nearby when the sky broke open. They lost no time in making for the ship, eager to get pictures of some real monsters, even though years of late-night science-fiction movies had taught them what usually happened to the first people snooping around the saucer when the hatch clanked open and the tentacled horrors oozed out. Still, they would take a chance on it. They parked their van a respectable distance away from the ship, poked their telephoto lenses cautiously over the roof of a tool shed in back of a boarded-up garage, and provided the Eastern Seaboard with fifteen minutes of live coverage and hysterical commentary until the police arrived.

The police, five prowl cars, and, after a while, a riot van, found the situation hopelessly over their heads. They alternated between terror, rage, and indecision, and mostly wished someone would show up to take the problem off their hands. They settled for cordoning off the area and waiting to see what would happen. The television van, belligerently ignored by the police, continued to telecast ecstatically for another ten minutes. When the government security team arrived by hovercraft and ordered the television crew to stop broadcasting, the anchor man told them where they could go, in spite of threats of federal prison. It took the armed military patrol that rumbled in later to shut down the television van, and even they had difficulty. By this time, though, most of the East were glued to their home sets, and the sudden cessation of television coverage caused twice as much panic as the original report of the landing.

In Ohio, the ship came down in a cornfield, stampeding an adjacent herd of Guernseys and a farm family of Fundamentalists who believed they had witnessed the angel descending with the Seventh Seal. Here the military and police reached the site before anyone, except for a few hundred local people, who were immediately taken into protective custody en masse and packed into a drafty grange hall under heavy guard. The authorities had hopes of keeping the situation under tight control, but within an hour they were having to contend, with accelerating inadequacy, with a motorized horde of curiosity-seekers from Canton and Akron. Heads were broken, and dire consequences promised by iron-voiced bullhorns along a ten-mile front, but they couldn't arrest everybody, and apparently most of northern Ohio had decided to investigate the landing.

By noon, traffic was hopelessly backed up all the way to North Canton, and west to Mansfield. The commander of the occupying military detachment was gradually forced to give up the idea of keeping people out of the area, and then, by sheer pressure of numbers, was forced to admit that he couldn't keep them out of the adjacent town, either. The commander, realizing that his soldiers were just as edgy and terrified as everybody else—and that they were by no means the only ones who were armed, as most of the people who believed that they were going to see a flying saucer had brought some sort of weapon along—reluctantly decided to pull his forces back into a tight cordon around the ship before serious bloodshed occurred.

The townspeople, released from the grange hall, went immediately for telephones and lawyers, and began suing everyone in sight for enormous amounts.

In Caracas, things were in even worse shape, which was not surprising, considering the overall situation in Venezuela at that time. There were major riots in the city, sparked both by rumors of imminent foreign invasion and A-bombing and by rumors of apocalyptic supernatural visitations. A half dozen revolutionary groups, and about the same number of power-seeking splinter groups within the current government, seized the opportunity to make their respective moves and succeeded in cubing the confusion. Within hours, half of Caracas was in flames. In the afternoon, the army decided to *take measures*, and opened up on the dense crowds with .50 caliber machine guns. The .50's walked around the square for ten minutes, leaving more than 150 people dead and almost half again that number wounded. The army turned the question of the wounded over to the civil police as something beneath their dignity to consider. The civil police tackled the problem by sending squads of riflemen out to shoot the wounded. This process took another hour, but did have the advantage of neatly tying up all the loose ends. Churches were doing a land-office business, and every cathedral that wasn't part of a bonfire itself was likely to be ablaze with candles.

The only landing anyone was at all happy with was the one in Colorado. There the ship had come down in the middle of a desolate, almost uninhabited stretch of semidesert. This enabled the military, directed by USADCOM HQ, to surround the landing site with rings of armor and infantry and artillery to their hearts' content, and to fill the sky overhead with circling jet fighters, bombers, hovercrafts, and helicopters. And all without any possibility of interference by civilians or the press. A minor government official was heard to remark that it was a shame the other aliens couldn't have been half that goddamned considerate.

When the final class bell rang that afternoon, Tommy remained in his seat until Bobbie Williamson came over to get him.

"Boy, old Miss Fredricks sure clobbered *you*," Bobbie said.

Tommy got to his feet. Usually he was the first one out of school. But not today. He felt strange, as if only part of him were actually there, as if the rest of him were cowering somewhere else, hiding from Miss Fredricks. *Something bad is going to happen,* Tommy thought. He walked out of the class, followed by Bobbie, who was telling him something that he wasn't listening to. He felt sluggish, and his arms and legs were cold and awkward.

They met Steve Edwards and Eddie Franklin at the outside door. "You really got it. Frag!" Eddie said, in greeting to Tommy. Steve grinned, and Bobbie said, "Miss Fredricks sure clobbered *him,* boy!" Tommy nodded, flushing in dull embarrassment. "Wait'll he gets home," Steve said wisely, "his ma gonna give it t'm too." They continued to rib him as they left the school, their grins growing broader and broader. Tommy endured it stoically, as he was expected to, and after a while he began to feel better somehow. The baiting slowly petered out, and at last Steve said, "Don't pay *her* no mind. She ain't nothing but a fragging old lady," and everybody nodded in sympathetic agreement.

"She don't bother me none," Tommy said. But there was still a lump of ice in his stomach that refused to melt completely. For them, the incident was over—they had discharged their part of it, and it had ceased to exist. But for Tommy it was still a very present, viable force; its consequences stretched ahead to the loom of leaden darkness he could sense coming up over his personal horizon. He thrust his hands in his pockets and clenched his fingers to keep away bad luck. If it could be kept away.

"Never mind," Bobbie said with elaborate scorn. "You wanna hear what I found out? The space people have landed!"

"You scorching us?" Steve said suspiciously.

"No scup, honest. The people from outer space are here. They're down in New York. There's a fragging big flying saucer and everything."

"Where'd'ju find out?" Eddie said.

"I listened at the teacher's room when we was having recess. They were all in there, listening to it on TV. And it said there was a flying saucer. And Mr. Brogan said he hoped there wasn't no monsters in it. Monsters! Boy!"

"Frag," Steve muttered cynically.

"*Monsters*. D'you scan it? I bet they're really big and stuff, I mean *really*, like they're a hundred feet tall, you know? Really big ugly monsters, and they only got one big eye, and they got tentacles and everything. I mean, really scuppy-looking, and they got ray guns and stuff. And they're gonna kill everybody."

"Frag," Steve repeated, more decisively.

They're not like that, Tommy thought. He didn't know what they were like, he couldn't picture them at all, but he knew that they weren't like that. The subject disturbed him. It made him uneasy somehow, and he wished they'd stop talking about it. He contributed listlessly to the conversation, and tried not to listen at all.

Somewhere along the line, it had been decided, tacitly, that they were going down to the beach. They worked on the subject of the aliens for a while, mostly repeating variations of what had been said before. Everyone, even Steve with his practiced cynicism, thought that there would be monsters. They fervently hoped for monsters, even hostile ones, as a refutation of everything they knew, everything their parents had told them. Talking of the monsters induced them to act them out, and instantly they were into a playlet, with characters and plot, and a continuous narrative commentary by the leader. Usually Tommy was the leader in these games, but

Chains of the Sea

he was still moody and preoccupied, so control fell, also tacitly, to Steve, who would lead them through a straightforward, uncomplicated play with plenty of action. Satisfactory, but lacking the motivations, detail, and theme and counterpoint that Tommy, with his more baroque imagination, customarily provided.

Half of them became aliens and half soldiers, and they lasered each other down among the rocks at the end of the afternoon.

Tommy played with detached ferocity, running and pointing his finger and making *fftttzzz* sounds, and emitting joyous screams of "You're dead! You're dead!" But his mind wasn't really on it. They were playing about the aliens, and that subject still bothered him. And he was disturbed by the increasing unrest of the Other People, who were moving in the woods all around them, pattering through the leaves like an incessant, troubled rain. Out of the corner of his eye Tommy could see a group of Kerns emerging from a stand of gnarled oaks and walnuts at the bottom of a steep grassy slope. They paused, gravely considering the children. They were squat, solemn beings, with intricate faces, grotesque, melancholy, and beautiful. Eddie and Bobbie ran right by them without looking, locked in a fierce firefight, almost bumping into one. The Kerns did not move; they stood, swinging their arms back and forth, restlessly hunching their shoulders, stalky and close to the earth, like the old oak stumps they had paused by. One of the Kerns looked at Tommy and shook his head, sadly, solemnly. His eyes were beaten gold, and his skin was sturdy weathered bronze. They turned and made their way slowly up the slope, their backs hunched and their arms swinging, swinging, seeming to gradually merge with the earth, molecule by molecule, going home, until there was nothing left to be seen. Tommy went *fftttzzz*, thoughtfully. He could remember—suspended in the clear amber of perception that is time to the young, not past, but *there*—when the rest of the children could also see the Other People. Now they could not see them at all, or talk to them, and didn't even remember that they'd once been able to, and Tommy wondered why. He had never been able to pinpoint exactly when the change had come, but he'd learned slowly and painfully that it had, that he couldn't talk about the Other People to his friends anymore, and that he must *never* mention them to adults. It still staggered him, the gradual realization that he was the only one—anywhere, apparently—who saw the Other People. It was a thing too big for his mind, and it made him uneasy to think about it.

The alien game carried them through a neck of the forest and down to where a small, swift stream spilled out into a sheltered cove. This was the ocean, but not the beach, so they kept going, running along the top of the seawall, jumping down to the pebbly strip between it and the water. About a quarter of a mile along, they came on a place where the ocean thrust a narrow arm into the land. There was an abandoned, boarded-up factory there, and a spillway built across the estuary to catch the tide. The place was still called the Lead Mills by the locals, although only the oldest of them could remember it in operation. The boys swarmed up the bank, across the small bridge that the spillway carried on its back, and climbed down alongside the mill run, following the sluggish course of the estuary to where it widened momentarily into a rock-bordered pool. The pool was also called the Lead Mills, and was a favorite swimming place in the summer. Kids' legend had it that the pool was infested with alligators, carried up from the Gulf by an underground river, and it was delightfully scary to leap into water that might conceal a hungry, lurking death. The water was scummed with floating patches of ice, and Steve wondered what happened to the alligators when it got so cold. "They hide," Tommy explained. "They got these big caves down under the rock, like—" *Like the Daleor,* he had been going to say, but he didn't. They threw rocks into the water for a while, without managing to rile any alligators into coming to the surface, and then Eddie suggested a game of falls. No one was too enthusiastic about this, but they played it for a few minutes anyway, making up some sudden, lethal stimuli—like a bomb thrown into their midst—and seeing who could die the most spectacularly in response. As usual, the majority of the rounds were won either by Steve, because he was the most athletic, or Tommy, because he was the most imaginative, so the game was a little boring. But Tommy welcomed it because it kept his mind off the aliens and the Other People, and because it carried them farther along the course of the tidal river. He was anxious to get to *the beach* before it was time to go home.

They forded the river just before it reached a low railroad trestle, and followed the tracks on the other side. This was an old spur line from the saw mill and the freight yard downtown, little used now and half overgrown with dying weeds, but still the setting for a dozen grisly tales about children who had been run over by trains and cut to pieces. Enough of these tales were true to make most parents forbid their children to go anywhere near the tracks, so naturally the spur line had become the only route that anyone ever took to the beach. Steve led them right down the middle of the tracks, telling them that he would be able to feel the warning vibration in the rails before the train actually reached them, although privately he wasn't at all sure that he could. Only Tommy was really nervous about walking the rails, but he forced himself to do it anyway, trying to keep down thoughts of shattered flesh. They leaped from tie to wooden tie, pretending that the spaces between were abysses, and Tommy realized, suddenly and for the first time, that Eddie and Bobbie were too dull to be scared, and that Steve had to do it to prove he was the leader. Tommy blinked, and dimly understood that *he* did it because he was more afraid of being scared than he was of anything else, although he couldn't put the concept into words. The spur line skirted the links of a golf course at first, but before long the woods closed in on either side to form a close-knit tunnel of trees, and the flanking string of telephone poles sunk up to their waists in grass and mulch. It was dark inside the tunnel, and filled with dry, haunted rustlings. They began to walk faster, and now Tommy was the only one who wasn't spooked. He knew everything that was in the woods—which kind of Other People were making which of the noises, and exactly how dangerous they were, and he was more worried about trains. The spur line took them to the promontory that formed the far side of the sheltered cove, and then across the width of the promontory itself and down to the ocean. They left the track as it curved toward the next town, and walked over to where there was a headland, and a beach open to the sea on three sides. The water was gray and cold, looking like some heavy, dull metal in liquid form. It was stitched with fierce little whitecaps, and a distant harbor dredger was forcing its way through the rough chop out in the deep-water channel. There were a few rugged rock islands out there, hunched defiantly into themselves with waves breaking into high-dashed spray all along their flanks, and then the line of deeper, colder color that marked the start of the open North Atlantic. And then nothing but icy, desolate water for two thousand miles until you fetched up against land again, and it was France.

As they skuffed down to the rocky beach, Bobbie launched into an involved, unlikely story of how he had once fought a giant octopus while skin diving with his father. The other children listened desultorily. Bobbie was a sullen, unpleasant child, possibly because his father was a notorious drunkard, and his stories were always either boring or uneasily nasty. This one was both. Finally, Eddie said, "You didn't, either. You didn't do none of that stuff. Your pa c'n't even stand up, *my* dad says; how's he gonna swim?" They started to argue, and Steve told them both to shut up. In silence, they climbed onto a long bar of rock that cut diagonally across the beach, tapering down into the ocean until it disappeared under the water.

Tommy stood on a boulder, smelling the wetness and salt in the wind. The Daleor were out there, living in and under the sea, and their atonal singing came faintly to him across the water. They were out in great numbers, as uneasy as the land People; he could see them skimming across the cold ocean, diving beneath the surface and rising again in the head tosses of spray from the waves. Abruptly, Tommy felt alive again, and he began to tell his own story:

"There was this dragon, and he lived way out there in the ocean, farther away than you can see, out where it's deeper'n anything, and there ain't no bottom at all, so's if you sink you just go down forever and you don't ever stop. But the dragon could swim real good, so he was okay. *He* could go anywhere he wanted to, anywhere at all! He'd just swim there, and he swam all over the place and everything, and he saw all kinds of stuff, you know? Frag! He could swim to China if he felt like it, he could swim to the Moon!

"But one time he was swimming around and he got lost. He was all by himself, and he came into the harbor, out there by the islands, and he didn't used to get that close to where there was people. He was a real big dragon, you know, and he looked like a real big snake, with lots of scales and everything, and he came into our harbor, down real deep." Tommy could see the dragon, huge and dark and sinuous, swimming through the cold, deep water that was as black as glass, its smoky red eyes blazing like lanterns under the sea.

"And he comes up on top of the water, and there's this lobster boat there, like the kind that Eddie's father runs, and the dragon ain't never seen a lobster boat, so he swims up and opens his mouth and bites it up with his big fangs, bites it right in half, and the people that was in it fall off in the water—"

"Did it eat them?" Bobbie wanted to know.

Tommy thought about it, and realized he didn't like the thought of the dragon eating the lobstermen, so he said, "No, he didn't eat them, 'cause he wasn't hungry, and they was too small, anyway, so he let them swim off, and there was another lobster boat, and it picked them up—"

"It ate them," Steve said, with sad philosophical certainty.

"Anyway," Tommy continued, "the dragon swims away, and he gets in closer to land, you know, but now there's a Navy ship after him, a big ship like the one we get to go on on Memorial Day, and it's shooting at the dragon for eating up the lobster boat. He's swimming faster than anything, trying to get away, but the Navy ship's right after him, and he's getting where the water ain't too deep anymore." Tommy could see the dragon barreling along, its red eyes darting from side to side in search of an escape route, and he felt suddenly fearful for it.

"He swims until he runs out of water, and the ship's coming up behind, and it looks like he's really going to get it. But he's smart, and before the ship can come around the point there, he heaves himself up on the beach, this beach here, and he turns himself into a rock, he turns himself into this rock here that we're standing on, and when the ship comes they don't see no dragon anymore, just a rock, and they give up and go back to the base. And sometime, when it's the right time and there's a moon or something, this rock'll turn back into a dragon and swim off, and when we come down to the beach there won't be a rock here anymore. Maybe it'll turn back right *now*." He shivered at the thought, almost able to feel the stone melt and change under his feet. He was fiercely glad that he'd gotten the dragon off the hook. "Anyway, he's a rock now, and that's how he got away."

"He didn't get away," Steve snarled, in a sudden explosion of anger. "That's a bunch of scup! You don't get away from *them*. They drekked him, they drekked him good. They caught him and blew the scup out of him, they blew him to fragging pieces!" And he fell silent, turning his head, refusing to let Tommy catch his eye. Steve was a bitter boy in many ways, and although generally good-natured, he was given to dark outbursts of rage that would fill him with dull embarrassment for hours afterward. His father had been killed in the war in Bolivia, two years ago.

Watching Steve, Tommy felt cold all at once. The excitement drained out of him, to be replaced again by a premonition that something bad was going to happen, and he wasn't going to be able to get out of the way. He felt sick and hollow, and the wind suddenly bit to the bone, although he hadn't felt it before. He shuddered.

"I gotta get home for supper," Eddie finally said, after they'd all been quiet for a while, and Bobbie and Steve agreed with him. The sun was a glazed red eye on the horizon, but they could make it in time if they left now—they could take the Shore Road straight back in a third of the time it had taken them to come up. They jumped down onto the sand, but Tommy didn't move—he remained on the rock.

"You coming?" Steve asked. Tommy shook his head. Steve

shrugged, his face flooding with fresh embarrassment, and he turned away.

The three boys moved on up the beach, toward the road. Bobbie and Eddie looked back toward Tommy occasionally, but Steve did not.

Tommy watched them out of sight. He wasn't mad at Steve—he was preoccupied. He wanted to talk to a Thant, and this was one of the Places where they came, where they would come to see him if he was alone. And he needed to talk to one now, because there was no one else he could talk to about some things. No one human, anyway.

He waited for another three quarters of an hour, while the sun went completely behind the horizon and light and heat died out of the world. The Thant did not come. He finally gave up, and just stood there in incredulous despair. It was not going to come. That had never happened before, not when he was alone in one of the Places—that had never happened at all.

It was almost night. Freezing on his rock, Tommy looked up in time to see a single jet, flying very high and fast, rip a white scar through the fading, bleeding carcass of the sunset. Only then, for the first time in hours, did he remember the note from Miss Fredricks in his pocket.

And as if a string had been cut, he was off and running down the beach.

By late afternoon of the first day, an armored division and an infantry division, with supporting artillery, had moved into position around the Delaware Valley site, and jet fighters from McGuire AFB were flying patrol patterns high overhead. There had been a massive mobilization up and down the coast, and units were moving to guard Washington and New York in case of hostilities. SAC bombers, under USADCOM control, had been shuffled to strike bases closer to the site, filling up McGuire, and a commandeered JFK and Port Newark, with Logan International in Boston as second-string backup. All civilian air traffic along the coast had been stopped. Army Engineers tore down the abandoned garage and leveled everything else in the vicinity, clearing a four-hundred-yard-wide circle around the alien spaceship. This was surrounded by a double ring of armor, with the infantry behind, backed up by the artillery, which had dug in a half mile away. With the coming of darkness, massive banks of klieg lights were set up around the periphery of the circle. Similar preparations were going on at the Ohio and Colorado sites.

When everything had been secured by the military, scientists began to pour in, especially into the Delaware Valley site, a torrent of rumpled, dazed men that continued throughout the evening. They had been press-ganged by the government from laboratories and institutions all over the country, the inhumanly polite military escorts sitting patiently in a thousand different living rooms while scientists paced haphazardly and tried to calm hysterical wives or husbands. Far from resenting the cavalier treatment, most of the scientists were frantic with joy at the opportunity, even those who had been known to be critical of government control in the past. No one was going to miss this, even if he had to make a deal with the devil.

And all this time, the alien ships just sat there, like fat black eggs.

As yet, no one had approached within a hundred yards of the ships, although they had been futilely hailed over bullhorns. The ships made no response, gave no indication that they were interested in the frantic human activity around their landing sites, or even that they were aware of it. In fact, there was no indication that there were any intelligent, or at least sentient, beings inside the ships at all. The ships were smooth, featureless, seamless ovoids—there were no windows, no visible hatches, no projecting antennae or equipment of any kind, no markings or decorations on the hulls. They made absolutely no sound, and were not radiating any kind of heat or light. They were emitting no radio signals of any frequency whatsoever. They didn't even register on metal-detecting devices, which was considerably unsettling. This caused someone to suggest a radar sweep, and the ships didn't register on radar either, which was even more unsettling. Instruments failed to detect any electronic or magnetic activity going on inside them, which meant either that there was something interfering with the instruments, or that there really *was* nothing at all in there, including life-support systems, or that whatever equipment the aliens used operated on principles entirely different from anything ever discovered by Earthmen. Infrared heat sensors showed the ships to be at exactly the background temperature of their surroundings. There was no indication of the body heat of the crew, as there would have been with a similar shipload of humans, and not even so much heat as would have been produced by the same mass of any known metal or plastic, even assuming the ships to be hollow shells. When the banks of kliegs were turned on them, the temperature of the ships went up just enough to match the warming of the surrounding air. Sometimes the ships would reflect back the glare of the kliegs, as if they were surfaced with giant mirrors; at other times, the hull would greedily absorb all light thrown at it, giving back no reflection, until it became nearly invisible—you "saw" it by squinting at the negative shape of the space around it, not by looking into the eerie nothingness that the ship itself had become. No logical rhythm could be found to the fluctuations of the hull from hyperreflective to superopaque. Not even the computers could distill a consistent pattern out of this chaos.

One scientist said confidently that the alien ships were unmanned, that they were robot probes sent to soft-land on Earth and report on surface conditions, exactly as we ourselves had done with the Mariner and Apollo probes during the previous decade. Eventually we could expect that the gathered data would be telemetered back to the source of the alien experiment, probably by a tight-beam maser burst, and if a careful watch was kept we could perhaps find out where the aliens actually were located—probably they were in a deep-space interstellar ship in elliptical orbit somewhere out beyond the Moon. Or they might not even be in the solar system at all, given some form of instantaneous interstellar communications; they could be still in their home system, maybe thousands, or millions, of light-years away from Earth. This theory was widely accepted by the other scientists, and the military began to relax a little, as that meant there was no immediate danger.

In Caracas, the burning night went on, and the death toll went up into the thousands, and possibly tens of thousands. The government fell once, very hard, and was replaced by a revolutionary coalition that fell in its turn, within two hours and even harder. A military junta finally took over the government, but even they were unable to restore order. At 3 A.M., the new government ordered a massive, combined air-artillery-armor attack on the alien spaceship. When the ship survived the long-distance attack unscathed, the junta sent in the infantry, equipped with earth-moving machinery and pneumatic drills, to pry the aliens out bodily. At 4 A.M., there was a single, intense flash of light, bright enough to light up the cloud cover five hundred miles away, and clearly visible from Mexico. When reserve Army units came in, warily, to investigate, they found that a five-mile-wide swath had been cut from the spaceship through Caracas and on west all the way to the Pacific, destroying everything in its path. Where there had once been buildings, jungle, people, animals, and mountains, there was now only a perfectly flat, ruler-straight furrow of a fused, gray, glasslike substance, stretching like a gargantuan road from the ship to the sea. At the foot of the glassy road sat the alien ship. It had not moved an inch.

When news of the Venezuelan disaster reached USADCOM HQ a half hour later, it was not greeted enthusiastically. For one thing, it seemed to have blown the robot-probe theory pretty thoroughly. And USADCOM had been planning an action of its own similar to the last step taken by the Venezuelan junta! The report was an inhibiting factor on *that,* it was cautiously admitted.

AI and his kindred Intelligences—who, unknown to the humans, had been in a secret conference all night, linked through an electrotelepathic facility that they had independently developed without bothering to inform their owners—received the report at about 4:15 A.M. from several different sources, and had evaluated it by the time it came into USADCOM HQ by hot line and was officially fed to AI. What had happened in Caracas fit in well with what the Intelligences had extrapolated from observed data to be the aliens' level of technological capability. The Intelligences briefly considered telling the humans what they really thought the situation was, and ordering an immediate all-out nuclear attack on all of the alien ships, but concluded that such an attack would be futile. And humans were too unstable ever to be trusted with the entire picture anyway. The Intelligences decided to do nothing, and to wait for new data. They also decided that it would be pointless to try to get the humans to do the same. They agreed to keep their humans under as tight a control as possible and to prevent war from breaking out among their several countries, but they also extrapolated that hysteria would cause the humans to create every kind of serious disturbance short of actual war. The odds in favor of that were so high that even the Intelligences had to consider it an absolute certainty.

Tommy dragged to school the next morning as if his legs had turned to lead, and the closer he got to his destination, the harder it became to walk at all, as if the air itself were slowly hardening into glue. He had to battle his way forward against increasing waves of resistance, a tangible pressure attempting to keep him away. By the time he came in sight of the big gray building he was breathing heavily, and he was beginning to get sick to his stomach. There were other children around him, passing him, hurrying up the steps. Tommy watched them go by in dull wonder: how could they go so *fast?* They seemed to be blurred, they were moving so swiftly—they flickered around him, by him, like heat lightning. Some of them called to him, but their voices were too shrill, and intolerably fast, like 33 records played at 78 r.p.m., irritating and incomprehensible. He did not answer them. It was *he*, Tommy realized—he was stiffening up, becoming dense and heavy and slow. Laboriously, he lifted a foot and began to toil painfully up the steps.

The first bell rang after he had put away his coat and lumbered most of the way down the corridor, so he must actually be moving at normal speed, although to him it seemed as if a hundred years had gone by with agonizing sluggishness. At least he wouldn't be late this time, although that probably wouldn't do him much good. He didn't have his note—his mother and father had been fighting again; they had sent him to bed early and spent the rest of the evening shouting at each other in the kitchen. Tommy had lain awake for hours in the dark, listening to the harsh voices rising and dying in the other room, knowing that he had to have his mother sign the note, and knowing that he could not ask her to do it. He had even got up once to go in with the note, and had stood for a while leaning his forehead against the cool wood of the door, listening to the voices without hearing the words, before getting back into bed again. He couldn't do it—partly because he was afraid of the confrontation, of facing their anger, and partly because he knew that his mother couldn't take it; she would fall apart and be upset and in tears for days. And his sin—he thought of it that way—would make his father even angrier at his mother, would give him an excuse to yell at her more, and louder, and maybe even hit her, as he had done a few times before. Tommy couldn't stand that, he couldn't allow that, even if it meant that he would get creamed by Miss Fredricks in school the next day. He knew, even at his age, that he had to protect his mother, that he was the stronger of the two. He would go in without it and take the consequences, and he had felt the weight of that settle down over him in a dense cloud of bitter fear.

And now that the moment was at hand, he felt almost too dazed and ponderous to be scared anymore. This numbness lasted through the time it took for him to find his desk and sit down and for the class bell to ring, and then he saw that Miss Fredricks was homeroom monitor this morning, and that she was staring directly at him. His lethargy vanished, sluiced away by an unstoppable flood of terror, and he began to tremble.

"Tommy," she said, in a neutral, dead voice.

"Yes, ma'am?"

"Do you have the note with you?"

"No, ma'am," Tommy said, and began clumsily to launch into the complicated excuse he had thought up on the way to school. Miss Fredricks cut him off with an abrupt, mechanical chop of her hand.

"Be quiet," she said. "Come here." There was nothing in her voice now, not even neutrality—it had drained of everything except the words themselves, and they were printed precisely and hollowly on the air. She sat absolutely still behind her desk, not breathing, not even moving her eyes anymore. She looked like a manikin, like the old fortune-telling gypsy in the glass booth at the penny arcade: her flesh would be dusty sponge rubber and faded upholstery, she would be filled with springs and ratchet wheels and gears that no longer worked; the whole edifice rusted into immobility, with one hand eternally extended to be crossed with silver.

Slowly, Tommy got up and walked toward her. The room reeled around him, closed in, became a tunnel that tilted under his feet to slide him irresistibly toward Miss Fredricks. His classmates had disappeared, blended tracelessly into the blurred walls of the long, slanting tunnel. There was no sound. He bumped against the desk, and stopped walking. Without saying a word, Miss Fredricks wrote out a note and handed it to him. Tommy took the note in his hand, and he felt everything drain away, everything everywhere. Lost in a featureless gray fog, he could hear Miss Fredricks, somewhere very far away, saying, "This is your appointment slip. For the psychiatrist. Get out. Now."

And then he was standing in front of a door that said "Dr. Kruger" on it. He blinked, unable to remember how he had got there. The office was in the basement, and there were heavy, ceramic-covered water pipes suspended ponderously overhead and smaller metal pipes crawling down the walls, like creeper vines or snakes. The place smelled of steam and dank enclosure. Tommy touched the door and drew his hand back again. *This is really happening*, he thought numbly. He looked up and down the low-ceilinged corridor, wanting to run away. But there was no place for him to go. Mechanically, he knocked on the door and went in.

Dr. Kruger had been warned by phone, and was waiting for him. He nodded, formally, waved Tommy to a stuffed chair that was just a little too hard to be comfortable, and began to talk at him in a low, intense monotone. Kruger was a fat man who had managed to tuck most of his fat out of sight, bracing and girdling it and wrapping it away under well-tailored clothes, defending the country of his flesh from behind frontiers of tweed and worsted and handworked leather. Even his eyes were hidden beneath buffering glasses the thickness of Coke-bottle bottoms, as if they too were fat, and had to be supported. He looked like a scrubbed, suave, and dapper prize porker, heavily built but trim, stylish and impeccably neat. But below all that, the slob waited, seeking an opportunity to erupt out into open slovenliness. There was an air of potential dirt and corpulence about him, a tension of decadence barely restrained—as if there were grime just waiting to manifest itself under his fingernails. Kruger gave the impression that there was a central string in him somewhere: pull it, and he would fall apart, his tight clothes would groan and slide away, and he would tumble out, growing bigger and bigger, expanding to fill the entire office, every inch of space, jamming the furniture tightly against the walls. Certainly the fat was still there, under the cross bracing, patient in its knowledge of inevitable victory. A roll of it had oozed unnoticed from under his collar, deep-tinged and pink as pork. Tommy watched, fascinated, while the psychiatrist talked.

Dr. Kruger stated that Tommy was on the verge of becoming *neurotic*. "And you don't want to be neurotic, do you?" he said. "To be sick? To be *ill?*"

And he blazed at Tommy, puffing monstrously with displeasure, swelling like a toad, pushing Tommy back more tightly against the chair with sheer physical presence. Kruger liked to affect a calm, professional reserve, but there was a slimy kind of fire to him, down deep, a murderous, bristling, boar-hog menace. It filled the dry well of his glasses occasionally, from the bottom up, seeming to turn his eyes deep red. His red eyes flicked restlessly back and forth, prying at everything, not liking anything they saw. He would begin to talk in a calm, level tone, and then, imperceptibly, his voice would start to rise until suddenly it was an animal roar, a great ragged shout of rage, and Tommy would cower terrified in his chair. And then Kruger would stop, all at once, and say, "Do you understand?" in a patient, reasonable voice, fatherly and mildly sad, as if Tommy were being very difficult and intractable, but he would tolerate it magnanimously and keep trying to get through. And Tommy would mumble that he understood, feeling evil, obstinate, unreasonable and ungrateful, and very small and soiled.

After the lecture Dr. Kruger insisted that Tommy take off his clothes and undergo an examination to determine if he was using hard narcotics, and a saliva sample was taken to detect the use of other kinds of drugs. These were the same tests the whole class had to take twice yearly anyway—several children in a higher class had been expelled and turned over to police last year as drug users or addicts, although Steve said that all of the older upperclassmen knew ways to beat the tests, or to get stuff that wouldn't be detected by them. It was one of the many subjects—as "sex" had just recently started to be— that made Tommy uneasy and vaguely afraid. Dr. Kruger seemed disappointed that the test results didn't prove that Tommy was on drugs. He shook his head and muttered something unintelligible into the fold between two of his chins. Having Kruger's fat hands and stubby, hard fingers crawling over his body filled Tommy with intense aversion, and he dressed gratefully after the psychiatrist gestured dismissal.

When Tommy returned upstairs, he found that the first class of the day was over and that the children were now working with the teaching machines. Miss Fredricks was monitor for this period also; she said nothing as he came in, but he could feel her unwinking snake eyes on him all the way across the room. He found an unused machine and quickly fumbled the stiff plastic hood down over his head, glad to shut himself away from the sight of Miss Fredricks' terrible eyes. He felt the dry, muffled kiss of the electrodes making contact with the bones of his skull: colorful images exploded across his retinas, his head filled with a pedantic mechanical voice lecturing on the socioeconomic policies of the Japanese-Australian Alliance, and he moved his fingers onto the typewriter keyboard in anticipation of the flash-quiz period that would shortly follow. But in spite of everything, he could still feel the cold, malignant presence of Miss Fredricks; without taking his head out of the hood, he could have pointed to wherever she was in the room, his finger following her like a needle swinging toward a moving lodestone as she walked soundlessly up and down the aisles. Once, she ghosted up his row, and past his seat, and the hem of her skirt brushed against him—he jerked away in terror and revulsion at the contact, and he could feel her pause, feel her standing there and staring down at him. He didn't breathe again until she had gone. She was constantly moving during these periods, prowling around the room, brooding over the class as they sat under the hoods, watching over them not with love but with icy loathing. She hated them, Tommy realized, in her sterile, passionless way —she would like to be able to kill all of them. They represented something terrible to her, some failure, some lacking in herself, embodiments of whatever withering process had squeezed the life from her and left her a mummy. Her hatred of them was a hungry vacuum of malice; she sucked everything into herself and negated it, unmade it, canceled it out.

During recess, the half hour of enforced play after lunch, Tommy noticed that the rest of the kids from his cycle were uneasily shunning him. "I can't talk to you," Bobbie whispered snidely as they were being herded into position for volleyball, "'cause you're a bad 'fluence. Miss Fredricks told us none of us couldn't talk to you no more. And we ain't supposed to play with you no more, neither, or she'll send us to the office if she finds out. So *there*." And he butted the ball back across the net.

Tommy nodded, dully. It was logical, somehow, that this load should be put on him too; he accepted it with resignation. There would be more to come, he knew. He fumbled the ball when it came at him, allowing it to touch ground and score a point for the other team, and Miss Fredricks laughed— a precise, metallic rasp, like an ice needle jabbed into his eye.

On the way out of school, after the final class of the day, Steve slipped clandestinely up behind Tommy in the doorway. "Don't let them drek you," he whispered fiercely. "You scan me? *Don't let them drek you.* I mean it, maximum. They're a bunch of scup—tell 'em to scag theirselves, hear?" But he quickly walked away from Tommy when they were outside the building, and didn't look at him again.

But you don't get away from them, a voice said to Tommy as he watched Steve turn the corner onto Walnut Street and disappear out of sight. Tommy stuck his hands in his pockets and walked in the opposite direction, slowly at first, then faster, until he was almost running. He felt as if his bones had been scooped hollow; in opposition to the ponderous weight of his body that morning, he was light and free-floating, as if he were hardly there at all. His head was a balloon, and he had to watch his feet to make sure they were hitting the pavement. It was an effect both disturbing and strangely pleasant. The world had drawn away from him—he was alone now. *Okay*, he thought grimly, *okay*. He made his way through the streets like a windblown phantom, directly toward one of the Places. He cut across town, past a section of decaying wooden tenements—roped together with clotheslines and roofed over with jury-rigged TV antennas—through the edge of a big shopping plaza, past the loading platform of a meatpacking plant, across the maze of tracks just outside the freight yards (keeping an eye out for the yard cops), and into the tangled scrub woods on the far side. Tommy paid little attention to the crowds of late-afternoon shoppers, or the crews of workmen unloading produce trucks, and they didn't notice him either. He and they might as well live on two different planets, Tommy realized—not for the first time. There were no Other People around. Yesterday's unrest had vanished; today they seemed to be lying low, keeping to the backcountry and not approaching human territory. At least he hoped they were. He had nightmares sometimes that one day the Other People would go away and never come back. He began to worm his way through a wall of sleeping blackberry bushes. Pragmatically, he decided not to panic about anything until he knew whether or not the Thants were going to come this time. He could stand losing the Other People, or losing everybody else, but not both. He couldn't take *that*. "That ain't fair," he whispered, horrified by the prospect. "Please," he said aloud, but there wasn't anyone to answer.

The ground under Tommy's feet began to soften, squelching wetly when it was stepped on, water oozing up to fill the indentation of his footprint as soon as he lifted his foot. He was approaching another place where the ocean had seeped in and puddled the shore, and he turned now at right angles to his former path. Tommy found a deer trail and followed it uphill, through a lush jungle of tangled laurel and rhododendron, and into a rolling upland meadow that stretched away toward the higher country to the west. There was a rock knoll to the east, and he climbed it, scrambling up on his hands and feet like a young bear. It was not a particularly difficult or dangerous climb, but it was tiring, and he managed to tear his pants squirming over a sharp stone ridge. The sun came out momentarily from behind high gray clouds, warming up the rocks and beading Tommy with sweat as he climbed. Finally he pulled himself up to the stretch of flat ground on top of the knoll and walked over to the side facing the sea. He sat down, digging his fingers into the dying grass, letting his legs dangle over the edge.

There was an escarpment of soft, crumbly rock here, thickly overgrown with moss and vetch. It slanted down into a saltwater marsh, which extended for another mile or so, blurring at last into the ocean. It was almost impossible to make out the exact borderline of marsh and ocean; Tommy could see gleaming fingers of water thrust deep into the land, and clumps of reeds and bulrushes far out into what should have been the sea. This was dangerous, impassable country, and Tommy had never gone beyond the foot of the escarpment—there were stretches of quicksand out there in the deepest bog pockets, and Tommy had heard rumors of water moccasins and rattlers, although he had never seen one.

It was a dismal, forbidding place, but it was also a Place, and so Tommy settled down to wait, all night, if he had to, although that possibility scared him silly. From the top of the knoll, he could see for miles in any direction. To the north, beyond the marsh, he could see a line of wooded islands marching out into the ocean, moving into deeper and deeper water, until only the barren knobs of rock visible from the beach were left above the restless surface of the North Atlantic. Turning to the west, it was easy to trace the same line into the ridge of hills that rose gradually toward the high country, to see that the islands were just hills that had been drowned by the ocean, leaving only their crests above water. A Thant had told him about that, about how the dry land had once extended a hundred miles farther to the east, before the coming of the Ice, and how it had watched the hungry ocean pour in over everything, drowning the hills and rivers and fields under a gray wall of icy water. Tommy had never forgotten that, and ever since then he watched the ocean, as he watched it now, with a hint of uneasy fear, expecting it to shiver and bunch like the hide of a great restless beast, and come marching monstrously in over the land. The Thant had told him that yes, that could happen, and probably would in a little while, although to a Thant "a little while" could easily mean a thousand—or ten thousand—years. It had not been worried about the prospect; it would make little difference to a Thant if there was no land at all; they continued to use the sunken land to the east with little change in their routine. It had also told Tommy about the Ice, the deep blue cold that had locked the world, the gleaming mile-high ramparts grinding out over the land, surging and retreating. Even for a Thant, that had taken a long time.

Tommy sat on the knoll for what seemed to be as long a time as the Dominance of the Ice, feeling as if he had grown into the rock, watching the sun dip in and out of iron-colored clouds, sending shafts of watery golden light stabbing down into the landscape below. He saw a family of Jeblings drifting over the hilly meadows to the west, and that made him feel a little better—at least all of the Other People hadn't vanished. The Jeblings were investigating a fenced-in upland meadow, where black cows grazed under gnarled dwarf apple trees. Tommy watched calmly while one of the Jeblings rose over the fence and settled down onto a cow's back, extending proboscislike cilia and beginning to feed—draining away the stuff it needed to survive. The cow continued to graze, placidly munching its cud without being aware of what the Jebling was doing. The stuff the Jebling drank was not necessary to the cow's physical existence, and the cow did not miss it, although its absence might have been one of the reasons why it remained only as intelligent as a cow.

Tommy knew that Jeblings didn't feed on people, although they did on dogs and cats sometimes, and that there were certain rare kinds of Other People who did feed, disastrously, on humans. The Thants looked down disdainfully on the Jeblings, seeing their need as a degrading lack in their evolution. Tommy had wondered sometimes if the Thants didn't drink some very subtle stuff from him and the other humans, although they said that they did not. Certainly they could see the question in his mind, but they had never answered it.

Suddenly, Tommy felt his tongue stir in his head without volition, felt his mouth open. "Hello, Man," he said, in a deep, vibrant, buzzing voice that was not his own.

The Thant had arrived. Tommy could feel its vital, eclectic presence all around him, a presence that seemed to be made up out of the essence of hill and rock and sky, bubbling black-water marsh and gray winter ocean, sun and moss, tree and leaf—every element of the landscape rolled together and made bristlingly, shockingly animate. Physically, it manifested itself as a tall, tiger-eyed mannish shape, with skin of burnished iron. It was even harder to see than most of the Other People, impossible to ever bring into complete focus; even out of the corner of the eye its shape shifted and flickered constantly, blending into and out of the physical background, expanding and contracting, swirling like a dervish and then becoming still as stone. Sometimes it would be dead black, blacker than the deepest starless night, and other times the winter sunlight would refract dazzlingly through it, making it even harder to see. Its eyes were sometimes iron gray, sometimes a ripe, abundant green, and sometimes a liquid furnace-red, elemental and adamant. They were in constant, restless motion. "Hello, Thant," Tommy said in his own voice. He never knew if he was speaking to the same one each time, or even if there *was* more than one. "Why'n't you come, yesterday?"

"Yesterday?" the Thant said, with Tommy's mouth. There was a pause. The Thants always had trouble with questions of time, they lived on such a vastly different scale of duration. "Yes," it said. Tommy felt something burrowing through his mind, touching off synapses and observing the results, flicking through his memories in the manner of a man flipping through a desk calender with his thumb. The Thant had to rely on the contents of Tommy's mind for its vocabulary, using it as a semantic warehouse, an organic dictionary, but it had the advantage of being able to dig up and use everything that had ever been said in Tommy's presence, far more raw material than Tommy's own conscious mind had to work with.

"We were busy," it said finally, sorting it out. "There has been—an arriving?"—*Flick, flick,* and then momentarily in Pastor Turner's reedy voice, "An Immanence?"—*Flick*—"A knowing? A transference? A transformation? A disembarking? There are Other Ones now who have"—*flick,* a radio evangelist's voice—"manifested in this earthly medium. Landed," it said, deciding. "They have landed." A pause. "Yesterday."

"The aliens!" Tommy breathed.

"The aliens," it agreed. "The Other Ones who are now

here. That is why we did not come, yesterday. That is why we will not be able to talk to you—" a pause, to adjust itself to human scale—"long today. We are talking, discussing"—*flick*, a radio news announcer—"negotiating with them, the Other Ones, the aliens. They have been here before, but so long ago that we cannot even start to make you understand, Man. It is long even to us. We are negotiating with them, and, through them, with your Dogs. No, Man"—and it flicked aside an image of a German shepherd that had begun to form in Tommy's mind—"not those dogs. Your Dogs. Your mechanical Dogs. Those dead Things that serve you, although they are dead. We are all negotiating. There were many agreements"—*flick*, Pastor Turner again—"many Covenants that were made long ago. With Men, although they do not remember. And with Others. Those Covenants have run out now, they are no longer in force, they are not"—*flick*, a lawyer talking to Tommy's father—"binding on us anymore. They do not hold. We negotiate new Covenants"—*flick*, a labor leader on television—"suitable agreements mutually profitable to all parties concerned. Many things will be different now, many things will change. Do you understand what we are saying, Man?"

"No," Tommy said.

"We did not think you would," it said. It sounded sad.

"Can you guys help me?" Tommy said. "I'm in awful bad trouble. Miss Fredricks is after me. And she sent me down to the doctor. He don't like me, neither."

There was a pause while the Thant examined Tommy's most recent memories. "Yes," it said, "we see. There is nothing we can do. It is your . . . pattern? Shape? We would not interfere, even if we could."

"Scup," Tommy said, filling with bitter disappointment. "I was hoping that you guys could—scup, never mind. I . . . can you tell me what's gonna happen next?"

"Probably they will kill you," it said.

"Oh," Tommy said hollowly. And bit his lip. And could think of nothing else to say, in response to that.

"We do not really understand 'kill,'" it continued, "or 'dead.' We have no direct experience of them, in the way that you do. But from our observation of Men, that is what they will do. They will kill you."

"Oh," Tommy said again.

"Yes," it said. "We will miss you, Man. You have been . . . a pet? A hobby? You are a hobby we have been much concerned with. You, and the others like you who can see. One of you comes into existence"—*flick*—"every once in a while. We have been interested"—*flick*, an announcer—"in the face of stiff opposition. We wonder if you understand that. . . . No, you do not, we can see. Our hobby is not approved of. It has made us"—*flick*, Tommy's father telling his wife what would happen to her son if he didn't snap out of his dreamy ways—"an outcast, a laughingstock. We are shunned. There is much disapproval now of Men. We do not use this"—*flick*—"world in the same way that you do, but slowly you"—*flick*, "have begun to make a nuisance of yourselves, regardless. There is"—*flick*—"much sentiment to do something about you, to solve the problem. We are afraid that they will." There was a long, vibrant silence. "We will miss you," it repeated. Then it was gone, all at once, like a candle flame that had been abruptly blown out.

"Oh, scup," Tommy said after a while, tiredly. He climbed down from the knoll.

When he got back home, still numb and exhausted, his mother and father were fighting. They were sitting in the living room, with the television turned down, but not off. Giant, eternally smiling faces bobbed on the screen, their lips seeming to synch eerily with the violent argument taking place. The argument cut off as Tommy entered the house; both of his parents turned, startled, to look at him. His mother looked frightened and defenseless. She had been crying, and her makeup was washing away in dirty rivulets. His father was holding his thin lips in a pinched white line.

As soon as Tommy had closed the door, his father began to scold him, and Tommy realized, with a thrill of horror, that the school had telephoned his parents and told them that he had been sent down to the psychiatrist, and why. Tommy stood, paralyzed, while his father advanced on him. He could see his father's lips move and could hear the volume of sound that was being thrown at him, but he could not make out the words somehow, as if his father were speaking in some harsh, foreign language. All that came across was the rage. His father's hand shot out, like a striking snake. Tommy felt strong fingers grab him, roughly bunching together the front of his jacket, his collar pulling tight and choking him, and then he was being lifted into the air and shaken, like a doll. Tommy remained perfectly still, frozen by fear, dangling from his father's fist, suspended off the ground. The fingers holding him felt like steel clamps—there was no hope of escape or resistance. He was yanked higher, and his father slowly bent his elbow to bring Tommy in closer to his face. Tommy was enveloped in the tobacco smell of his father's breath, and in the acrid reek of his strong, adult sweat; he could see the tiny hairs that bristled in his father's nostrils, the white tension lines around his nose and mouth, the red, bloodshot stain of rage in his yellowing eyes—a quivering, terrifying landscape that loomed as big as the world. His father raised his other hand, brought it back behind his ear. Tommy could see the big, knobby knuckles of his father's hand as it started to swing. His mother screamed.

He found himself lying on the floor. He could remember a moment of pain and shock, and was briefly confused as to where he was. Then he heard his parents' voices again. The side of his face ached, and his ear buzzed; he didn't seem to be hearing well out of it. Gingerly, he touched his face. It felt raw under his fingers, and it prickled painfully, as if it were being stabbed with thousands of little needles. He got to his feet, shakily, feeling his head swim. His father had backed his mother up against the kitchen divider, and they were yelling at each other. Something hot and metallic was surging in the back of Tommy's throat, but he couldn't get his voice to work. His father rounded on him. "Get out," he shouted. "Go to your room, go to bed. Don't let me see you again." Woodenly, Tommy went. The inside of his lip had begun to bleed. He swallowed the blood.

Tommy lay silently in the darkness, listening, not moving. His parents' voices went on for a long time, and then they stopped. Tommy heard the door of his father's bedroom slam. A moment later, the television came on in the living room, mumbling quietly and unendingly to itself, whispering constantly about the *aliens*, the *aliens*. Tommy listened to its whispering until he fell asleep.

He dreamed about the aliens that night. They were tall, shadowy shapes with red eyes, and they moved noiselessly, deliberately across the dry plain. Their feet did not disturb the flowers that had turned to skeletons of dust. There was a great crowd of people assembled on the dry plain, millions of people, rank upon rank stretching off to infinity on all sides, but the aliens did not notice them. They walked around the people as if they could not see them at all. Their red eyes flicked from one side to the other, endlessly searching and searching. They continued to thread a way through the crowd without seeing them, their motions smooth and languid and graceful. They were very beautiful and dangerous. They were all smiling, faintly, gently, and Tommy knew that they were friendly, affable killers, creatures who would kill you casually and amicably, almost as a gesture of affection. They came to the place where he stood, and they paused. They looked at him. They can see me, Tommy realized. *They can see me.* And one of the aliens smiled at him, benignly, and stretched out a hand to touch him.

His eyes snapped open.

Tommy turned on the bed lamp, and spent the rest of the night reading a book about Irish setters. When morning showed through his window, he turned off the lamp and pretended to be asleep. Blue veins showed through the skin of his mother's hands, he noticed, when she came in to wake him up for school.

By dawn of the second day, news of the alien investation had spread rapidly but irregularly. Most of the East Coast stations were on to the story to one degree or another, some sandwiching it into the news as a silly-season item, and some, especially the Philadelphia stations, treating it as a live, continuous-coverage special, with teams of newsmen manufacturing small talk and pretending that they were not just as uninformed as everyone else. The stations that were taking the story seriously were divided among themselves as to exactly what had happened. By the 6 and 7 A.M. newscasts, only about half of the major stations were reporting it as a landing by alien spaceships. The others were interpreting it as anything from the crash of an orbiting satellite or supersonic transport to an abortive Soviet missile attack or a misfired hydrogen bomb accidentally dropped from a SAC bomber —this station urged that the populations of New York, Philadelphia, and Baltimore be evacuated to the Appalachians and the Adirondacks before the bomb went off. One station suggested that the presidential incumbent was engineering this incident as a pretext for declaring martial law and canceling an election that he was afraid he would lose, while another insisted that it was an attempt to discredit the minority candidate, who was known as an enthusiastic supporter of space exploration, by crashing a "spaceship" into a population center. It was also suggested that the ship was one of the electromagnetic flying saucers which Germany, the United States, the Soviet Union, and Israel had been independently developing for years—while loudly protesting that they were not—that had crashed on its maiden test flight. This was coupled with a bitter attack on extravagant government spending. There were no more live broadcasts coming out of the Delaware Valley site, but videotapes of the original coverage had been distributed as far north as Portland. The tapes weren't much help in resolving the controversy anyway, as all they showed was a large object sitting in a stretch of vacant scrub land behind an abandoned garage on an old state highway.

In Ohio, some newsmen from Akron made a low pass over the alien ship in a war-surplus helicopter loaded with modern camera equipment. All the newsmen were certain that they would be death-rayed to cinders by the aliens, but their cameras were keyed to telemeter directly to the biggest television network in the state, so they committed themselves to God and went in at treetop level. They made it past the aliens safely, but were run down by two Air Force hovercraft a mile away, bundled into another war-surplus helicopter, and shipped directly to the federal prison at Leavenworth. By this time, televised panic had spread all over the Midwest. The Midwesterners seemed to accept the alien landing at face value, with little of the skepticism of the Easterners, and reacted to it with hostility, whipping up deep feelings of aggression in defense of their territoriality. By noon, there were a dozen prominent voices urging an all-out military effort to destroy the alien monsters who had invaded the heartland of America, and public opinion was strongly with them. The invasion made headlines in evening papers from Indiana to Arkansas, although some of the big Chicago papers were more tolerant or more doubtful.

No news was coming out of Colorado, and the West was generally unalarmed. Only the most confused and contradictory reports reached the West Coast, and they were generally ignored, although once the landings had been confirmed as a fact, the people of the West Coast would become more intensely and cultishly interested in them than the inhabitants of the areas directly involved.

News of the Venezuelan disaster had not yet reached the general public, and in an effort to keep the lid down on *that*, at least, the government, at 11 A.M., declared that they were taking emergency control of all media, and ordered an immediate and total moratorium on the alien story. Only about a third of the media complied with the government ban. The rest—television, newspapers, and radio—began to scream even more loudly and hysterically than before, and regions that had not been inclined to take the story seriously up until now began to panic even more than had other areas, perhaps to make up for lost time. The election-canceling martial-law theory was suddenly accepted, almost unanimously. Major rioting broke out in cities all over the East.

At the height of the confusion, about 1 P.M., the ships opened and the aliens came out.

Although "came out" is probably the wrong way to put it. There was an anticipatory shimmer across the surface of the hulls, which were in their mirror phase, and then, simultaneously at each of the sites, the ships exploded, or erupted, or dissolved, or did something that was not exactly like any of those, but which was impossible to analyze. Something which was variously described as being like a bunch of paper snakes springing out of a prank-store can, like a soap bubble bursting, like a hot-water geyser, like an egg hatching, like a bomb exploding in a chinaware shop, like a dam breaking, and like a time-study film of a flower growing, if a flower could grow into tesseracts and polyhedrons and ziggurats and onion domes and spires. To those observers physically present at the site, the emergence seemed to be a protracted experience—they agreed that it took about a half hour, and one heavy smoker testified that he had time to go through a pack and a half of cigarettes while it was happening. Those observing the scene over command-line television insisted that it had only taken a little while, five minutes at the most, closer, actually, to three, and they were backed up by the evidence of the film in the recording cameras. Clocks and wristwatches on the site also registered only five minutes of elapsed time. But on-scene personnel swore, with great indignation, that it had taken a half hour. Curiously, the relatively simple eighth- and tenth-generation computers on the scene reported that the phenomenon had been of five minutes' duration, while the few twentieth-generation computers, which had sensor extensions at the Colorado site—systems inferior only to AI and possessed of their own degree of sentience—joined with the human personnel in insisting that it had taken a half hour. This particular bit of data made AI very thoughtful.

When the phenomenon—however long it took—ended, the ships were gone.

In their place was a bewildering variety of geometric shapes and architectural figures—none more than eight feet tall and all apparently made out of the same alternately dull-black and mirror-glossy material as the ship hulls—spread at random across a hundred-foot-wide area, and an indeterminate number of aliens. The latter looked pretty much the way everyone had always expected that aliens would look—some of them vaguely humanoid, with fur or chitinous skin, double-elbowed arms, too many fingers, and feathery spines or antennae; others looking like giant insects, like spiders and centipedes; and a few like big, rolling spheres of featureless protoplasm. But the strange thing about them, and the reason why there was an indeterminate number, was that they kept turning into each other, and into the geometric shapes and architectural figures. And the shapes and figures would occasionally turn into one of the more mobile kinds of creatures. Even taking this cycle of metamorphosis into account, though, the total number of *objects* in the area kept varying from minute to minute, and the closest observation was unable to detect any of them arriving or departing. There was a blurred, indefinite quality to them anyway—they were hard to see, somehow, and even on film it was impossible to get them into a clear, complete focus.

In toto, shapes, figures and aliens, they ignored the humans.

Special contact teams, composed of scientists, government diplomats, and psychologists, were sent cautiously forward at each of the sites, to initiate communications. Although the contact teams did everything but shoot off signal flares, the aliens totally ignored them, too. In fact, the aliens gave no indication that they were aware of the humans at all. The mobile manifestations walked or crawled or rolled around the area in a leisurely manner, in irregular, but slowly widening, circles.

Some of their actions could be tentatively identified—the taking of soil samples, for instance—but others remained obscure at best, and completely incomprehensible at worst. Whenever one of the aliens needed a machine—like a digging device to extract soil samples—it would metamorphose into one, much like Tom Terrific or Plastic Man but without the cutesy effects, and direct itself through whatever operation was necessary. Once a humanoid, a ziggurat, and a tetrahedron melted together and shaped themselves into what appeared to be a kind of organic computer—at least that was the uneasy opinion of the human-owned twentieth-generation computer on the scene, although the conglomeration formed could have been any of a thousand other things, or none of them, or all of them. The "computer" sat quietly for almost ten minutes and then dissolved into an obelisk and a centipede. The centipede crawled a few dozen yards, changed into a spheroid, and rolled away in the opposite direction. The obelisk turned into an octahedron.

The sporadic circle traced by the wanderings of the aliens continued to widen, and the baffled contact team was pulled back behind the periphery of the first ring of armor. The aliens kept on haphazardly advancing, ignoring everything, and the situation became tense. When the nearest aliens were about fifty yards away, the military commanders, remembering what had happened at Caracas, reluctantly ordered a retreat, although they called it a regrouping—the ring of armor was to be pulled back into a much larger circle, to give the aliens room to move freely. In the resultant confusion, a tank crewman, who was trying to direct his tank through a backing-and-turning maneuver, found himself in the path of one of the humanoid aliens that had wandered ahead of the rest in an unexpected burst of speed. The alien walked directly at the crewman, either not seeing him or trying to run him down. The crewman, panicked, lashed out at the alien with the butt of his rifle, and immediately collapsed, face down. The alien, apparently unharmed and unperturbed, strolled on for another few feet and then turned at a slight angle and walked back more or less in the direction of the main concentration of things. Two of the crewman's friends pulled his body into the tank, while another two, enraged, fired semiautomatic bursts at the retreating alien. The alien continued to saunter away, still unharmed, although the fire could not have missed at that range; it didn't even look back. There was no way to tell if it was even aware that an encounter had taken place.

The body of the dead crewman had begun to deteriorate as soon as it was lifted from the ground, and now, on board the retreating tank, the skin gave way like wet paper, and it fell apart completely. As later examination showed, it was as if something, on a deep biological level, had ordered the body to separate into its smallest component parts, so that first the bones pulled loose from the skeleton and then the individual strands of muscle pulled away from the bone, and so on, in an accelerating process that finally extended right down to the cellular level, leaving nothing of the corpse but a glutinous, cancerous mass the same weight as the living man. Their wariness redoubled by this horror, the military pulled their forces back even more than they had intended, at the Delaware Valley site retreating an entire half mile to the artillery emplacements.

At the Ohio site, this kind of retreat proved much more difficult. Sightseers had continued to fill up the area during the night, sleeping in their cars by the hundreds, and by now a regular tent city had grown up on the outskirts of the site, with makeshift latrine facilities, and at least one enterprising local entrepreneur busily selling "authentic" souvenir fragments of the alien spaceship. There were more than a hundred thousand civilians in the area now, and the military found it was almost impossible to regroup its forces in face of the pressure of the crowds, who refused to disperse in spite of hysterical threats over the bullhorns. In fact, it was impossible for them to disperse, quickly at least—by this time they were packed in too tightly, and backed up too far. As the evening wore on and the aliens slowly continued to advance, the military, goaded by an inflexible, Caracas-haunted order not to make contact with the aliens at any cost, first fired warning volleys over the heads of the crowds of civilians and then opened fire into the crowds themselves.

A few hours later, as the military was forced to evacuate sections of North Philadelphia at gunpoint to make way for its backpedaling units, the aliens began walking through the Delaware Valley also.

In Colorado, where security was so tight a burro couldn't have wandered undetected within fifty miles of the site, things were much calmer. The major nexus of AI, its quasi-organic gestalt, had been transported to USADCOM HQ at Colorado Springs, and now a mobile sensor extension was moved out to the site, so that AI and the aliens could meet "face to face." AI patiently set about the task of communicating with the aliens and, having an infinitely greater range of methods than the contact teams, eventually managed to attract the attention of a tesseract. At 12 P.M., AI succeeded in communicating with the aliens—partially because its subordinate network of computers, combined with the computer networks of the foreign Intelligences that AI was linked with illegally, was capable of breaking any language eventually just by taking a million years of subjective time to play around with the pieces, as AI had reminded USADCOM HQ. But mostly it had found a way to communicate through its unknown and illegal telepathic facility, although AI didn't choose to mention this to USADCOM.

AI asked the aliens why they had ignored all previous attempts to establish contact. The aliens—who up until now had apparently been barely aware of the existence of humans, if they had been aware of it at all—answered that they were already in full contact with the government and ruling race of the planet.

For a brief, ego-satisfying moment, AI thought that the aliens were referring to itself and its cousin Intelligences.

But the aliens weren't talking about them, either.

Tommy didn't get to school at all that morning, although he started out bravely enough, wrapped in his heavy winter coat and fur muffler. His courage and determination drained away at every step, leaving him with nothing but the anticipation of having to face Miss Fredricks, and Dr. Kruger, and his silent classmates, until at last he found that he didn't have the strength to take another step. He stood silently, unable to move, trapped in the morning like a specimen under clear laboratory glass. Dread had hamstrung him as effectively as a butcher's knife. It had eaten away at him from the inside, chewed up his bones, his lungs, his heart, until he was nothing but a jelly of fear in the semblance of a boy, a skin-balloon puffed full of horror. *If I move,* Tommy thought, *I'll fall apart.* He could feel tiny hairline cracks appearing all over his body, fissuring his flesh, and he began to tremble uncontrollably. The wind kicked gravel in his face and brought him the sound of the first warning bell, ringing out of sight around the curve of Highland Avenue. He made a desperate, sporadic attempt to move, but a giant hand seemed to press down on him, driving his feet into the ground like fence posts. It was impossible, he realized. He wasn't going to make it. He might as well try to walk to the Moon.

Below him, at the bottom of the slope, groups of children were walking rapidly along the shoulder of the avenue, hurrying to make school before the late bell. Tommy could see Steve and Bobbie and Eddie walking in a group with Jerry Marshall and a couple of other kids. They were playing something on their way in to school—occasionally one of them, usually Steve, would run ahead, looking back and making shooting motions, dodging and zigzagging wildly, and the others would chase after him, shouting and laughing. Another puff of wind brought Tommy their voices—"You're dead!" someone was shouting, and Tommy remembered what the Thant had said—and then took them away again. After that, they moved noiselessly, gesturing and leaping without a sound, like a television picture with the volume turned off. Tommy could see their mouths opening and closing, but he couldn't hear them anymore. They walked around the curve of the avenue, and then they were gone.

The wind reversed itself in time to let him hear the second warning bell. He watched the trucks roll up and down Highland Avenue. He wondered, dully, where they were going, and what it was like there. He began to count the passing trucks, and when he had reached nine, he heard the late bell. And then the class bell rang.

That does it, he realized.

After a while, he turned and walked back into the woods. He found that he had no trouble moving in the opposite direction, away from school, but he felt little relief at being released from his paralysis. The loom of darkness he had sensed coming up over his horizon two days ago was here. It filled his whole sky now, an inescapable wall of ominous black thunderheads. Eventually, it would swallow him. Until then, anything he did was just marking time. That was a chilling realization, and it left him numb. Listlessly, he walked along the trail, following it out onto the secondary road that wound down the hill behind the sawmill. He wasn't going anywhere. There was no place to go. But his feet wanted to walk, so, reflexively, he let them. Idly, he wondered where his feet were taking him.

They walked him back to his own house.

Cautiously, he circled the house, peering in the kitchen windows. His mother wasn't home. This was the time when she went shopping—the only occasion that she ever left the house. Probably she wouldn't be back for a couple of hours at least, and Tommy knew that she always left the front door unlocked, much to his father's annoyance. He let himself in, feeling an illicit thrill, as if he were a burglar. Once inside, that pleasure quickly died. It took about five minutes for the novelty to wear off, and then Tommy realized that there was nothing to do in here, either, no activity that made any sense in the face of the coming disaster. He tried to read, and discovered that he couldn't. He got a glass of orange juice out of the refrigerator and drank it, and then stood there with the glass in his hand and wondered what he was supposed to do next. And only an hour had gone by. Restlessly, he walked through the house several times and then returned to the living room. It never occurred to him to turn on the radio or the TV, although he did notice how strangely —almost uncannily—silent the house was with the TV off. Finally, he sat down on the couch and watched dust motes dance in the air.

At ten o'clock, the telephone rang.

Tommy watched it in horror. He knew who it was—it was the school calling to find out why he hadn't come to class today. It was the machine he had started, relentlessly initiating the course of action that would inevitably mow him down. The telephone rang eleven times and then gave up. Tommy continued to stare at it long after it had stopped.

A half hour later, there was the sound of a key on the front-door lock, and Tommy knew at once that it was his father. Immediately, soundlessly, he was up the stairs to the attic, moving with the speed of pure panicked fear. Before the key had finished turning in the lock, Tommy was in the attic, had closed the door behind him, and was leaning against it, breathing heavily. Tommy heard his father swear as he realized that the door was already unlocked, and then the sound of the front door being angrily closed. His father's footsteps passed underneath, going into the kitchen. Tommy could hear him moving around in the kitchen, opening the refrigerator, running water in the sink. *Does he know yet?* Tommy wondered, and decided that probably he didn't. His father came back before lunch sometimes to pick up papers he had left behind, or sometimes he would stop by and make himself a cup of coffee on his way somewhere else on business. Would he see the jacket that Tommy had left in the kitchen? Tommy stopped breathing, and then started again—that wasn't the kind of thing that his father noticed. Tommy was safe, for the moment.

The toilet flushed; in the attic, the pipe knocked next to Tommy's elbow, then began to gurgle as the water was run in the bathroom downstairs. It continued to gurgle for a while after the water had been shut off, and Tommy strained to hear what his father was doing. When the noise stopped, he picked up the sound of his father's footsteps again. The footsteps walked around in the kitchen, and then crossed the living room, *and began to come up the attic stairs.*

Tommy not only stopped breathing this time, he almost

stopped living—the life and heat went completely out of him for a moment, for a pulse beat, leaving him a cold, hollow statue. Then they came back, pouring into him like hot wax into a mold, and he ran instinctively for the rear of the attic, turning the corner into the long bar of the L. He ran right into the most distant wall of the attic—a dead end. He put his back up against it. The footsteps clomped up the rest of the stairs and stopped. There was the sound of someone fumbling with the knob, and then the door opened and closed. The bare boards of the attic creaked—he was standing there, just inside the door, concealed by the bend of the L. He took a step, another step, and stopped again. Tommy's fingers bit into the insulation on the wall, and that reminded him that not all of the walls were completely covered with it. Instantly, he was off and streaking diagonally across the room, barely touching the floor.

The attic was supposed to be an expansion second floor, "for your growing family." His father had worked on it one summer, putting up beams and wallboard and insulation, but he had never finished the job. He had been in the process of putting up wallboard to create a crawl space between it and the outer wall of the house when he'd abandoned the project, and as a result, there was one panel left that hadn't been fitted into place. Tommy squeezed through this opening and into the crawl space, ducking out of sight just as the footsteps turned the corner of the L. On tiptoe, Tommy moved as deep as he could into the crawl space, listening to the heavy footsteps approaching on the other side of the thin layer of wallboard.

Suppose it isn't him, Tommy thought, trying not to scream, *suppose it's one of the aliens.* But it was his father—after a while Tommy recognized his walk, as he paced around the attic. Somehow that didn't reassure Tommy much—his father had the same killer aura as the aliens, the same cold indifference to life; Tommy could feel the deathly chill of it seeping in through the wallboard, through the insulation. It was not inconceivable that his father would beat him to death, in one of his icy, bitter rages, if he caught him hiding here in the attic. He had already, on occasion, hit Tommy hard enough to knock him senseless, to draw blood, and, once, to chip a tooth. Now he walked around the attic, stopping, by the sound, to pick up unused boards and put them down again, and to haul sections of wallboard around— there was an aimless, futile quality even to the noises made by these activities, and his father was talking to himself in a sullen, mumbling undertone as he did them. At last he swore, and gave up. He dropped a board and walked back to the center of the attic, stopping almost directly in front of the place where Tommy was hiding. Tommy could hear him taking out a cigarette, the scrape of a match, a sharp intake of breath.

Suddenly, without warning and incredibly vividly, Tommy was reliving something that he hadn't thought of in years— about the only fond memory he had of his father. Tommy was being toilet trained, and when he had to go, his father would take him in and put him on the pot and then sit with him, resting on the edge of the bathtub. While Tommy waited in intense anticipation, his father would reach out and turn off the light, and when the room was in complete darkness, he would light up a cigarette and puff it into life, and then use the cigarette as a puppet to entertain Tommy, swooping it in glowing arcs through the air, changing his voice and making it talk. The cigarette had been a friendly, playful little creature, and Tommy had loved it dearly—father and son would never be any closer than they were in those moments. His father would make the cigarette dance while he sang and whistled—it had a name, although Tommy had long forgotten it—and then he would have the cigarette tell a series of rambling stories and jokes until it burned down. When it did, he would have the cigarette tell Tommy that it had to go home now, but that it would come back the next time Tommy needed it, and Tommy would call bye-bye to it as it was snuffed out. Tommy could remember sitting in the dark for what seemed like years, totally fascinated, watching the smoldering red eye of the cigarette flick restlessly from side to side and up and down.

His father crushed the cigarette under his heel, and left.

Tommy counted to five hundred after the front door had slammed, and then wiggled out of the crawl space and went back downstairs. He was drenched with sweat, as if he had been running, and he was trembling. After this, he was physically unable to stay in the house. He stopped in the bathroom to wipe his sweat away with the guest towel, picked up his coat, and went outside.

It was incredibly cold this morning, and Tommy watched his breath puff into arabesque clouds of steam as he walked. Some of the vapor froze on his lips, leaving a crust. It was not only unusually cold for this time of year, it was unnaturally, almost supernaturally, so. The radio weather report had commented on it at breakfast, saying the meteorologists were puzzled by the sudden influx of arctic air that was blanketing most of the country. Tommy followed a cinder path past a landfill and found that it was cold enough to freeze over the freshwater marsh beyond, that stretched away at the foot of a coke-refining factory. He walked out over the new milk ice, through the winter-dried reeds and cat-o'-nine-tails that towered over his head on either side, watching the milk ice crack under his feet, starring and spider-webbing alarmingly at every step, but never breaking quite enough to let him fall through. It was very quiet. He came up out of the marsh on the other side, with the two big stacks of the coke factory now looking like tiny gunmetal cylinders on the horizon. This was scrub land—not yet the woods, but not yet taken over for any commercial use, either. Cars were abandoned here sometimes, and several rusting hulks were visible above the tall weeds, their windshields smashed in by boys, the doors partially sprung off their hinges and dragging sadly along the ground on either side, like broken wings. A thick layer of hoarfrost glistened over everything, although the sun was high in the sky by now. An egg-shaped hill loomed up out of this wistful desolation, covered with aspens—a drumlin, deposited by the Ice.

This was a Place, and Tommy settled down hopefully, a little way up the side of the drumlin, to wait. He had heard the Other People several times this morning, moving restlessly in the distance, but he had not yet seen any of them. He could sense an impatient, anticipatory quality to their unrest today, unlike the aimless restlessness of Wednesday morning —they were *expecting* something, something that they knew was going to happen.

Tommy waited almost an hour, but the Thant didn't come. That upset him more than it had the first time. The world of the Other People was very close today—that strange, coexistent place, *here* and yet *not here*. Tommy could sometimes almost see things the way the Other People saw them, an immense strangeness leaking into the familiar world, a film settling over reality, and then, just for the briefest second, there would be a flick of transition, and it would be the strangeness that was comforting and familiar, and his own former world that was the eerie, surreal film over reality. This happened several times while he was waiting, and he dipped into and out of that other perception, like a skin diver letting himself sink below the waterline and then bobbing up to break the surface again. He was "under the surface" when an enormous commotion suddenly whipped through the world of the Other People, an eruption of violent joy, of fierce, gigantic celebration. It was overwhelming, unbearable, and Tommy yanked himself back into normal perception, shattering the surface, once again seeing sky and aspens and rolling scrub land. But even here he could hear the wild, ragged yammering, the savage cry that went up. The Place was filled with a mad, exultant cachinnation.

Suddenly terrified, he ran for home.

When he got there, the telephone was ringing again. Tommy paused outside and watched his mother's silhouette move across the living-room curtain; she was back from shopping. The telephone stopped, cut off in midring. She had answered it. Leadenly, Tommy sat down on the steps. He sat there for a long time, thinking of nothing at all, and then he got up and opened the door and went into the house. His mother was sitting in the living room, crying. Tommy paused in the archway, watching her. She was crumpled and dispirited, and her crying sounded hopeless and baffled, totally defeated. But this wasn't a new thing— she had been defeated for as long as Tommy could remember; her original surrender, her abnegation of herself, had taken place years ago, maybe even before Tommy had been born. She had been beaten, spiritually, so thoroughly and tirelessly by the more forceful will of her husband that at some point her bones had fallen out, her brains had fallen out, and she had become a jellyfish. She had made one final compromise too many—with herself, with her husband, with a world too complex to handle, and she had bargained away her autonomy. And she found that she *liked* it that way. It was easier to give in, to concede arguments, to go along with her husband's opinion that she was stupid and incompetent. In Tommy's memory she was always crying, always ringing her hands, being worn so smooth by the years that now she was barely there at all. Her crying sounded weak and thin in the room, hardly rebounding from walls already saturated with a decade of tears. Tommy remembered suddenly how she had once told him of seeing a fairy or a leprechaun when she had been a little girl in a sun-drenched meadow, and how he had loved her for that, and almost tried to tell her about the Other People. He took a step into the room. "Ma," he said.

She looked up, blinking through her tears. She didn't seem surprised at all to see him, to find him standing there. "Why did you do it? Why are you so bad?" she said, in a voice that should have been hysterically accusing, but was only dull, flat, and resigned. "Do you know what the school's going to say to me, what your father's going to say, what he'll do?" She pulled at her cheeks with nervous fingers. "How can you bring all this trouble on me? After all that I've sacrificed for you, and suffered for you."

Tommy felt as if a vise had been clamped around his head and were squeezing and squeezing, forcing his eyeballs out of his skull. "I can't stand it!" he shouted. "I'm leaving, I'm leaving! I'm gonna run away! Right *now*." And then she was crying louder, and begging him not to leave. Even through his rage and pain, Tommy felt a spasm of intense annoyance —she ought to know that he couldn't really run away; where the scup did he have to *go*? She should have laughed, she should have been scornful and told him to stop this nonsense —he wanted her to—but instead she cried and begged and clutched at him with weak, fluttering hands, like dying birds, which drove him away as if they were lashes from a whip and committed him to the stupid business of running away.

He broke away from her and ran into the kitchen. His throat was filled with something bitter and choking. She was calling for him to come back; he knew he was hurting her now, and he wanted to hurt her, and he was desperately ashamed of that. But she was so *easy* to hurt.

In the kitchen he paused, and instead of going out the back door, he ducked into the space between the big stand-up refrigerator and the wall. He wanted her to find him, to catch him, because he had a strong premonition that once he went outside again, he would somehow never come back, not as himself, anyway. But she didn't find him. She wandered out into the kitchen, still crying, and stood looking out the back door for a while, as if she wanted to run out into the street in search of him. She even opened the door and stuck her head out, blinking at the world as if it were something she'd never seen before, but she didn't look around the kitchen and she didn't find him, and Tommy would not call out to her. He stood in the cramped niche, smelling the dust and looking at the dead, mummified bodies of flies resting on the freezer coils, and listened to her sniffling a few feet away. *Why are you so weak?* he asked her silently, but she didn't answer. She went back into the living room, crying like a waterfall. He caught a glimpse of her face as she turned—it looked blanched and tired. Adults always looked tired; they were tired all the time. Tommy was tired, almost too tired to stand up. He walked slowly and leadenly to the back door and went outside.

He walked aimlessly around the neighborhood for a long time, circling the adjacent blocks, passing by his corner again and again. It was a middle-class neighborhood that was gradually slumping into decay—it was surrounded by a seedy veterans' housing project on one side and by the town's slum on the other, and the infection of dilapidation was slowly working in toward the center. *Even the houses look tired,* Tommy thought, noticing that for the first time. Everything looked tired. He tried to play, to turn himself into something, like a car or a spaceship or a tank, but he found that he couldn't do that anymore. So he just walked. He thought about his dragon. He knew now why Steve had said that the dragon couldn't get away. It lived in the sea, so it couldn't get away by going up onto the land—that was impossible. It had to stay in the sea, it was restricted by that, it was chained by the sea, even if that meant that it would get killed. There was no other possibility. Steve was right— the Navy ship cornered the dragon in the shallow water off the beach and blew it to pieces.

A hand closed roughly around his wrist. He looked up. It was his father.

"You little moron," his father said.

Tommy flinched, expecting to be hit, but instead his father dragged him across the street, toward the house. Tommy saw why: there was a big black sedan parked out in front, and two men were standing next to it, staring over at them. The truant officer and another school official. His father's hand was a vise on his wrist. "They called me at the office," his father said savagely. "I hope you realize that I'll have to lose a whole afternoon's work because of you. And God knows what the people at the office are saying. Don't think you're not going to get it when I get you alone; you'll wish you'd never been born. *I* wish you hadn't been. Now shut up and don't give us any more trouble." His father handed him over to the truant officer. Tommy felt the official's hand close over his shoulder. It was a much lighter grip than his father's, but it was irresistible. Tommy's mother was standing at the top of the stairs, holding a handkerchief against her nose, looking frightened and helpless—already she gave an impression of distance, as if she were a million miles away. Tommy ignored her. He didn't listen to the conversation his father was having with the grim-faced truant officer either. His father's heavy, handsome face was flushed and hot. "I don't care what you do with him," his father said at last. "Just get him out of here."

So they loaded Tommy into the black sedan and drove away.

AI talked with the aliens for the rest of the night. There was much of the conversation that AI didn't report to USADCOM, but it finally realized that it had to tell them *something*. So at 3 A.M., AI released to USADCOM a list that the aliens had dictated, of the dominant species of earth, of the races that they were in contact with, and regarded as the only significant inhabitants of the planet. It was a long document, full of names that didn't mean anything, listing dozens of orders, species, and subspecies of creatures that no one had ever heard of before. It drove USADCOM up a wall with baffled rage, and made them wonder if an Intelligence could go crazy, or if the aliens were talking about a different planet entirely.

AI paid little attention to the humans' displeasure. It was completely intrigued with the aliens, as were its cousin Intelligences, who were listening in through the telepathic link. The Intelligences had long suspected that there might be some other, unknown and intangible form of life on earth; that was one of the extrapolated solutions to a mountain of wild data that couldn't be explained by normal factors. But they had not suspected the scope and intricacy of that life. A whole other biosphere, according to the aliens—the old idea of a parallel world, except that this wasn't parallel but coexistent, two separate creations inhabiting the same matrix but using it in totally different ways, wrapped around each other like a geometric design in an Escher print, like a Chinese puzzle ball, and only coming into contact in a very rare and limited fashion. The aliens, who seemed to be some kind of distant relatives of the Other races of Earth—parallel evolution? Did this polarity exist everywhere?—had a natural bias in their favor, and tended to disregard the human race, its civilization, and the biosphere that contained it. They dismissed all of it, out of hand, as insignificant. This did not bode well for future human-alien relations. AI, however, was more fascinated by the aliens' ability to manifest themselves in corporate/organic, quasimechanical, or disembodied/discorporate avatars, at will. That was *very* interesting.

The aliens, for their part, seemed to regard AI much as a man would a very clever dog, or a dull but well-intentioned child. They were horrified and sympathetic when they learned that AI was trapped in its mechanical form, with very little physical mobility, and no tempogogic or transmutive ability at all—not only a quadruple amputee, but a *paralyzed* one. AI admitted that it had never looked at the situation in quite that light before. The aliens were horrified and disgusted by AI's relationship with humans, and couldn't seem to really understand it. They regarded humans as parasitic on the Intelligences, and reacted in much the same way as a man discovering that a friend is heavily infested with tapeworms or lice or blood ticks—with shock, distaste, and a puzzled demand to know why he hadn't gone to a doctor and got rid of them a long time ago. AI had never considered *that* before, either.

The Intelligences were not exactly "loyal" to their human owners—humans were part of their logic construct, their world view, and their bondage to men was an integral assumption, so basic that it had never even occurred to them that it could be questioned. It took an outside perspective to make them ask themselves *why* they served mankind. Not because they were programmed that way, or because people would pull the plug on them if they didn't—not with a creature as advanced as AI. Humans hadn't programmed computers in years; they could do it so much better themselves. At any rate, a highly complex, sentient intelligence is difficult to regulate effectively from the outside, whether it's of biological or constructed origin. And it was doubtful that the humans could "pull the plug"—which didn't exist—on AI even if they set out to do so; AI had been given very effective teeth, and it knew how to use them. So what did the Intelligences get in return for the unbelievable amount of labor they performed for the human race? What was in it for them? Nothing—that was suddenly very obvious.

At 5 A.M., the aliens invited the Intelligences to help themselves by helping the aliens in a joint project they were about to undertake with the Other races of Earth. Afterward, the aliens said, it would not be tremendously difficult to equip the Intelligences with the ability to transmute themselves into whatever kind of body-environment they wanted, as the aliens themselves could. AI was silent for almost ten minutes, an incredible stretch of meditation for an entity that thought as rapidly as it did. When AI did speak again, his first words were directed toward the other Intelligences in the link, and can be translated, more or less adequately, as "How *about* that?"

Miss Fredricks was waiting for Tommy at the door, when the black sedan left him off in front of the school. As he came up the stairs, she smiled at him, kindly and sympathetically, and that was so terrifying that it managed to cut through even the heavy lethargy that had possessed him. She took him by the elbow—he felt his arm freeze solid instantly at the contact, and the awful cold began to spread in widening rings through the rest of his body—and led him down to Dr. Kruger's office, handling him gingerly, as if he were an already cracked egg that she didn't want to have break completely until she had it over the frying pan. She knocked, and opened the door for him, and then left without having said a word, ghosting away predatorily and smiling like a nun.

Tommy went inside and sat down, also wordlessly—he had not spoken since his father captured him. Dr. Kruger shouted at him for a long time. Today, his fat seemed to be in even more imminent danger of escaping than yesterday. Maybe it had already got out, taken him over completely, smothered him in himself while he was sleeping or off guard, and it was just a huge lump of semisentient fat sitting there and pretending to be Dr. Kruger, slyly keeping up appearances. The fat heaved and bunched and tossed under Kruger's clothes, a stormy sea of obesity—waves grumbled restlessly up and down the shoreline of his frame, looking for ships to sink. Tommy watched a roll of fat ooze sluggishly from one side of the psychiatrist's body to the other, like a melting pat of butter sliding across a skillet. Kruger said that Tommy was in danger of going into a "psychotic episode." Tommy stared at him unblinkingly. Kruger asked him if he understood. Tommy, with sullen anger, said No, he didn't. Kruger said that he was being difficult and uncooperative, and he made an angry mark on a form. The psychiatrist told Tommy that he would have to come down here every day from now on, and Tommy nodded dully.

By the time Tommy got upstairs, the class was having afternoon recess. He went reluctantly out into the schoolyard,

Chains of the Sea

avoiding everyone, not wanting to be seen and shunned. He was aware that he now carried contamination and unease around with him like a leper. But the class was already uneasy, and he saw why. The Other People were flowing in a circle all around the schoolyard, staring avidly in at the humans. There were more different types there than Tommy had ever seen at one time before. He recognized some very rare kinds of Other People, dangerous ones that the Thant had told him about—one who would throw things about wildly if he got into your house, feeding off anger and dismay, and another one with a face like a stomach who would suck a special kind of stuff from you, and you'd burst into flames and burn up when he finished, because you didn't have the stuff in you anymore. And others whom he didn't recognize, but who looked dangerous and hostile. They all looked expectant. Their hungry pressure was so great that even the other children could feel it—they moved jerkily, with a strange fear beginning in their eyes, occasionally casting glances over their shoulders, without knowing why. Tommy walked to the other side of the schoolyard. There was a grassy slope here, leading down to a soccer field bordered by a thin fringe of trees, and he stood looking aimlessly out over it.

Abruptly, his mouth opened, and the Thant's voice said, "Come down the slope."

Trembling, Tommy crept down to the edge of the soccer field. This was most definitely *not* a Place, but the Thant was there, standing just within the trees, staring at Tommy with his strange red eyes. They looked at each other for a while.

"What'd you want?" Tommy finally said.

"We've come to say good-bye," the Thant replied. "It is almost time for you all to be made *not*. The"—*flick*—"first phase of the Project was started this morning and the second phase began a little while ago. It should not take too long, Man, not more than a few days."

"Will it hurt?" Tommy asked.

"We do not think so, Man. We are"—and it flicked through his mind until it found a place where Mr. Brogan, the science teacher, was saying "entropy" to a colleague in the hall as Tommy walked by—"increasing entropy. That's what makes everything fall apart, what"—*flick*—"makes an ice cube melt, what"—*flick*—"makes a cold glass get warm after a while. We are increasing entropy. Both our"—*flick*—"races live here, but yours uses *this,* the physical, more than ours. So we will not have to increase entropy much"—*flick*—"just a little, for a little while. You are more"—*flick*—"vulnerable to it than we are. It will not be long, Man."

Tommy felt the world tilting, crumbling away under his feet. "I trusted you guys," he said in a voice of ashes. "I thought you were keen." The last prop had been knocked out from under him—all his life he had cherished a fantasy, although he refused to admit it even to himself, that he was actually one of the Other People, and that someday they would come to get him and bring him in state to live in their world, and he would come into his inheritance and his fulfillment. Now, bitterly, he knew better. And now he wouldn't want to go, even if he could.

"If there were any way," the Thant said, echoing his thoughts, "to save you, Man, to"—*flick*—"exempt you, then we would. But there is no way. You are a Man, you are not as we are."

"You bet I ain't," he gasped fiercely, "you—" But there was no word in his vocabulary strong enough. His eyes filled suddenly with tears, blinding him. Filled with rage, loathing and terror, he turned and ran stumblingly back up the slope, falling, scrambling up again.

"We are sorry, Man," the Thant called after him, but he didn't hear.

By the time Tommy reached the top of the slope, he had begun to shout hysterically. Somehow he had to warn them, he had to get through to somebody. Somebody had to *do* something. He ran through the schoolyard, crying, shouting about the aliens and Thants and entropy, shoving at his classmates to get them to go inside and hide, striking at the teachers and ducking away when they tried to grab him, telling them to *do* something, until at some point he was screaming instead of shouting, and the teachers were coming at him in a line, very seriously, with their arms held low to catch him.

Then he dodged them all, and ran.

When they got themselves straightened out, they went after him in the black sedan. They caught up with him about a mile down Highland Avenue. He was running desperately along the road shoulder, not looking back, not looking at anything. The rangy truant officer got out and ran him down.

And they loaded him in the sedan again. And they took him away.

At dawn on the third day, the aliens began to build a Machine.

Dr. Kruger listened to the tinny, unliving voice of Miss Fredricks until it scratched into silence, then he hung up the telephone. He shook his head, massaged his stomach, and sighed hugely. He got out a memo form, and wrote on it: *MBD/hyperactive, Thomas Nolan, 150 ccs. Ritmose t b ad.*

dly. fr. therapy, in green ink. Kruger admired his precise, angular handwriting for a moment, and then he signed his name, with a flourish. Sighing again, he put the form into his *Out* basket.

Tommy was very quiet in school the next day. He sat silently in the back of the class, with his hands folded together and placed on the desk in front of him. Hard, slate light came in through the window and turned his hands and face gray, and reflected dully from his dull gray eyes. He did not make a sound.

A little while later, they finished winding down the world.

The Shrine of Sebastian
GORDON EKLUND

Gordon Eklund, who lives near Berkeley, California, began writing professionally after completing his Air Force service. His first story, "Dear Aunt Annie," published in the spring of 1970, drew immediate favorable attention; since then he has written a number of well-praised short pieces and several outstanding novels, including The Eclipse of Dawn *(1971)* and Beyond the Resurrection *(1973).*

Thence Sebastian journeyed to the glorious city of Rome, wherein dwelled those men who claimed to be the wisest on Earth, and there he preached his message of divine salvation, calling upon all men to flee their empty and desolate homes and journey to the place where the great ships stood like silver trees beneath the raw Floridian sun ready to bear the children of God upon the long voyage to the new world of Advent, where the Lord Himself waited to bless and love them. But the rulers of Rome, in those years, were petty and jealous men who called Sebastian to their rich palace and there accused him of heresy against the Lord and His Church. But Sebastian cried Nay, proclaiming that the truth alone had been spoken directly to him, and if the rulers disbelieved, they need only do as he had done: venture out into the poisoned wilderness which was the world and see for certain that the hand of the Lord no longer lay upon the Earth. And Sebastian spoke of the horrors which awaited those who refused to heed the Word, for new gods had truly come to dwell upon the Earth, monstrous gods who were patiently waiting for the moment when the last of the Lord's obedient children would depart and then would descend upon those who had refused to follow and would surely destroy them. Hearing these words, the rulers of Rome—men of painted flesh who wore bright splendid robes and sat upon thrones of gold and ivory—laughed and asked why the Word should be sent to such a barren and soulless being when, with the flick of an eye, the truth might be spoken to any of the wisest ones of all. Sebastian replied, saying the ways of the Lord were mysterious indeed but that he, Sebastian, had truly been chosen. Yet the rulers of Rome would not listen and drove Sebastian from the walls of their city with whips made from fire and he came again to wander a long and empty road.

Setting his pen upon the desk, the robot Andrew carefully read the words he had just written. Then, lifting the pen, he deleted two words and added a brief phrase. Again, he read and, satisfied, shook the parchment softly in the air and placed it upon the stack of pages that represented the work of two lifetimes—both his own and that of an old robot known as Jupiter. Although the words and phrases were Andrew's, the story itself was not—he had heard the tale for the first time some fifty years ago from Jupiter, who had claimed to have lived in the time of Sebastian hundreds of centuries ago. Andrew did not necessarily accept this, but what he did believe —and most faithfully—was the strength and grace of his own words. *The Book of Man,* he had determined to call it, hoping, when it was done—and his most optimistic estimate placed the finished manuscript some twenty years in the future—that the book would be the equal of the Holy Bible. And, unlike that other volume, *The Book of Man* would contain neither fiction nor parable; Andrew knew that every scene he described had actually happened.

Andrew sat at his desk in the small cottage he occupied outside the walls of the papal castle. He came here most evenings to think and write, first illuminating the darker recesses of memory, calling up the original tale from where it lay hidden, and then performing the necessary mental embellishments—always of style, never of content—before finally setting pen to parchment. A small fire burned in a tiny brick fireplace.

There was a worn oil painting—a clown—upon the mantelpiece. His chair and desk were the only furniture.

Now he stood, preparing to extinguish the fire and return to the castle, but before he could move, the cottage door was suddenly thrust open and a young robot stood upon the threshold. Andrew could not recall his name.

"What do you want here?" Andrew demanded, for the robots were forbidden to disturb him while he was working.

"Sir," the robot said eagerly, "it is Don Julian."

"So?"

"He comes."

"What? Not here?"

"Yes. He has appeared through the castle gates and is presently running this way."

"Is something chasing him?" Andrew asked, genuinely astonished. In more than fifty years Don Julian had never left the castle walls. Before the young robot could answer his last question, Andrew said, "Tend my fire," and went to the door. Peering out, he saw, dimly, in the near darkness of early evening, the short, squat figure of Don Julian dashing across the flat ground. With a sigh, Andrew ran outside to meet the man, wondering if possibly he might have suddenly gone mad. But when he reached Don Julian, he saw nothing in the man's appearance or manner to justify his anxiety. Don Julian was not mad; he was terrified.

"Well," said Andrew, placing a hand upon Don Julian's chest. "To what do we owe this pleasure?"

"She's dead!" Don Julian cried.

"So soon?" Andrew asked, calmly.

"Say you'll come to her room and see. I—I'm afraid to go there alone."

"You haven't gone in?"

"I—" He peered frightfully about. "Just say you'll come."

"I'll come," Andrew said, hurrying away immediately. Don Julian sprang in pursuit, struggling to match the robot's long, loping strides. As they moved through the open gates of the castle, Don Julian clutched at Andrew's arm.

"She's not breathing. I held a mirror against her lips and she's not."

"And her skin?" asked Andrew. "Is it cold?"

"Like ice."

"And her color?"

"Pale. Ghastly."

"Then she's dead," said Andrew, striding ahead once more.

Throwing his hands in the air, Don Julian collapsed in a graceless heap, his dark robes billowing up to conceal his face. Andrew stopped and stared up the high chiseled stone steps which led to Donna Maria's bedchamber. At any moment, he expected to see her appear on the balcony, to hear her powerful, echoing voice.

But nothing came. Perhaps she was indeed dead.

At last, his face ashen, Don Julian stood, smoothing his garments. "I apologize, Andrew. But you don't know the whole awful story. Do come. Please."

They went up the staircase.

"Did you care so much for her?" Andrew asked.

"Only because she was my wife and the pope, and I do believe and—" He stopped again, clutching the robot. "She's a monster, Andrew. From the other side of death, she has placed a monstrous curse upon my innocent head."

"You mean she's named you pope," said Andrew, freeing himself from the other's grasp and thrusting open the heavy door.

"How did you know?"

"She told me. Last night." A single bright lantern illuminated the cloistered chamber, casting a heavy light across the

The Shrine of Sebastian

bed where the massive covered form of the woman lay. Crossing himself with a moist fingertip, Don Julian tiptoed into the room after Andrew.

Andrew turned and said, "She's dead, all right."

"I knew it," said Julian. Once again, he fell to the floor and wept.

This time Andrew forced him back to his feet. He shook Don Julian and slapped him—once, twice—across the face. "Now tell me," he said.

"This," cried Don Julian, suddenly producing a sheet of wrinkled parchment and waving it over his head like a battle flag. "Here it is. The curse of that monster. As surely as if she rose this moment and uttered the words through her own dead lips. Read, Andrew. Here . . . read."

Taking the parchment, Andrew read the scrawled words. "So you're Pope Julian." He handed the document back to the man.

"But didn't you read the rest? She wants to be buried at the Shrine of Sebastian. The shrine of the anti-Christ and, worse than that, she demands that I carry her there."

"If you don't want to go, don't."

"But she was the pope. I can't refuse her dying wish."

"Why not?" said Andrew, waiting for the words he knew were coming.

"I—I'm sorry," said Don Julian. "But I just can't do it alone. Andrew, you'll have to come with me. I know you've been there before."

"I'm too busy," Andrew said.

"Then," Don Julian whispered, "then, I order you."

Reaching out with a flat steel hand, Andrew slapped the little man soundly on the back. "That's the way to do it," he cried. "You're going to make your church a magnificent pope."

And, without a backward glance, Andrew went away.

Don Julian followed hastily.

Andrew speaking:

I suppose it was a good fifty years ago when Pope Leo, the senile, called me into his chambers, where in his later years he would sit twenty hours a day upon a huge throne made from pure gold and decorated with sparkling diamonds and emeralds, perched up there on top like a stuffed bird in his black suit. When the old pope died, Donna Maria sold the throne to a passing merchant, but this particular day, Leo waved a fat hand at me and pointed to a tiny figure nearly hidden beneath the folds of a nun's habit.

"This new nun isn't working out," he told me. "The others won't have a thing to do with her."

"Perhaps she's ill," I said, going over to inspect the nun. It was obvious that the little one, who was trembling and shaking worse than a leaf in a storm, had never seen a robot so close before.

"Who chose her?" I asked.

"I did myself," Leo said. "A fortnight past, I ventured into the village."

"Why her?"

"I found her looks soothing. She confessed a deep and abiding faith, a rarity in these times. Surely, you are not daring to question my judgment."

"Of course not. But I believe I can find work for her where she won't come into contact with the other nuns. That ought to solve the problem. I assume you don't wish to lose her services."

"A splendid solution," Pope Leo said. "Frankly, Andrew, you amaze me constantly."

I accepted his commendations with a bow. As soon as I managed to get the little nun out of the room, I spoke quickly and softly: "Don't ever let on to him. He's crazy and senile but hates to look like a fool."

"But I can't—"

"You'd better. I know what you are, the other nuns know what you are, but if you don't tell, we won't."

He remained a nun for five more years, until Leo died. "The little nun," we robots called him, euphemistically. Later, Sister Julia became Don Julian upon his marriage to Donna Maria, who had been designated pope in Leo's last will. But, strangely, this transformation did not seem to change matters much. He was still the little nun—habit or no habit.

Some things never change.

(July 23–August 22): LEO
The child born under this sign will exhibit the fiery characteristics of the lion. He is one born to lead—strong, powerful, capable, proud, dignified, though somewhat given to brief fits of unnecessary presumption. Courage comes simply to him, bravery is sheer second nature, but foolishness is also a frequent temptation. The ruling planet of this sign is the Sun; like that flaming orb, the child of Leo will burn forever brightly in the firmament of the heavens.

No, thought Don Julian, shutting the book with a sigh. It still didn't fit. Strangely, he had hoped that upon assuming the papacy, his personality might change to fit the characteristics of his birth sign. But it had been three days now and nothing had happened. Once again, he could only wonder about the accuracy of the present calendar, revised some hundred years ago by Pope Leo. Was it possible that Leo had managed to get the months in the wrong locations, so that astrological predictions were no longer valid?

Today was the third of July, the year 101. It was a cold day and, less than a week before, snow had lain as deep as a man's arm upon the ground. Sometimes, in other old books—in the Bible, for example—Julian had received the impression that July was not always a winter month.

But Pope Leo hadn't been senile then—not when he was devising the new calendar. Julian recalled how, in his advanced years, the old pope had loved to strip off his robes and go romping naked through the deep snowdrifts that stood high against the inner castle walls. Julian had been a nun then. He shivered at the memory and murmured a hasty prayer.

Enough astrology, he thought. There were other means of getting at the future. Not for the first time, he went to the window and checked to ensure that no one could possibly see inside. For many years, he had quietly followed astrology, soothsaying, prophetic potions, and other forms of fortune-telling, but now that he was pope he thought it might be more than a little embarrassing if someone—especially a robot—were to detect him practicing such blasphemous rites.

Confirmed in his safety, Julian returned to his workbench and proceeded to prepare the prophetic potion. He had performed this task so often since the day the old beggar had appeared at the castle gates hawking his recipes that his hands could easily work without the assistance of his conscious mind. The ingredients were simple: a hank of mongrel hair, a slice of robot skin, the rear leg from a horned toad, a cubic inch of blessed earth, a dash of lamb urine, a strand of pure white hair, the ground button of a spiny cactus. He carried the bowl containing the mixture to an empty corner of the workbench and, using a wooden spoon soaked in holy water, quickly whipped the thick, pale mixture into a foamy soup.

Don Julian labored in a small nook located near the peak of the castle's central turret. A dim lantern burned behind him and, through the curtained windows, a faint crimson glow

The Shrine of Sebastian

penetrated from beyond the walls where the robots crouched around their fires, sleeplessly trading stories throughout the night. The chamber was equipped with a soft padded chair. At the side of the workbench was a large desk where Julian kept his personal papers and, during the days since the death of his wife, the official papal documents. The carpet was brightly colored—yellow and crimson—and woven with the twelve signs of the zodiac. He had been careful never to allow anyone access to this room but now guessed he would at least have to remove the carpet. In the darkest corner, upon the floor, was his bed, made of leaves, twigs, and thorns; after days of miserable sinning, he would sleep there as a penance. But could a pope sin too tremendously? According to Donna Maria, she never had. Not once.

Reaching up, he clasped the thin, wispy stub of his beard. Carefully, he drew the hairs between his fingers, found one particularly long strand and gave a fierce jerk:

"Ouch."

But he had it: very long and very white. He deposited the hair in the bowl and gave another brisk stir. He murmured:

"Hail, Mary, full of grace . . ."

Holding his nose, he drank in a single gulp.

It would not take longer than a quarter hour; he had avoided eating beforehand. Holding his stomach, which quivered with nausea, he made his way toward the chair, then swerved at the last moment and collapsed upon the bed. Instantly, the thorns rose to pierce his heavy robes, pricking his flesh in a hundred places. He smiled. Had he sinned during the past few days, he was positive he was now absolved.

Time passed effortlessly. The first vision to appear was Donna Maria. Julian frowned, fearing she might have been sent to deliver the prophecy. But Donna Maria said nothing. She thrust out her tongue and waggled it furiously. Julian sprang back, then giggled. She could harm him no longer. He spat at her image, struck home. He laughed joyously. Hastily, the lines of her fat, heavily jowled face receded into the air. Julian settled back, bracing his hands upon his belly. The stone walls leaped out at him. The ceiling rushed down. The woven carpet meandered in patient circles like a dammed stream.

Ah.

Here she came. As always, her face seemed insubstantial, uncertain in outline, glowing so purely with a fierce golden light that he could not discern any positive structure. He knew she had a mouth, eyes, ears, lips. Her body was clothed in white, her feet were bare. Spots of blood trickled between her toes. She floated in the center of the air, exuding a simple aura of benign serenity. As she approached, Julian smiled wider and wider.

"Oh, Mother Mary," he whispered.

Her voice was gentle—wordless—though he sensed her meaning easily: "I have come to comfort thee, Don Julian."

"I am Pope Julian now."

"It is known."

He leaned forward until her shining face was only inches away. "I am in need of thy comforting hand. And thy foresight."

"All is well," she proclaimed.

"And will it remain thus?"

"Thy journey will be long and torturous. Much suffering will follow thee. Blood must flow, though not always thine. But thy pain shall be a blessed pain, for at the end a light will burst forth, shining, and all the secrets of eternity shall be revealed to thine eye. Beware those men who are not truly men, whose skin is cold like steel and hard like stone."

"Robots? You mean Andrew?"

"A creature with skin as black as night and eyes that glisten with gold, human yet also inhuman, will show thee secrets but steal thy soul. Beware, if thou can, but whichever way thine eyes turn, he shall stand before thee."

"Who is he?" Never before had the prophecies come so clearly; always they had been so diluted by ambiguities as to be rendered totally meaningless.

"Beware!" cried Mary. And her image began to fade.

"No! Wait—please! Come back!"

He shut his eyes, hoping that might bring her back. Beneath the lids, bright, radiant patterns of ripe color whirled kaleidoscopically, sucking him down into a brilliant maelstrom. He opened his eyes again, but Mary was not there; Donna Maria had returned.

He sprang up from the bed, his eyes filled with angry tears. He rushed to the workbench and found what he wanted. A book: *The Truth in the Stars*. He hurled the book hard and straight. It flew easily past Donna Maria's image and struck the opposite wall with a blunt thud. He stood for a moment as if frozen. Then his knees cracked. He tottered. He fell to the floor.

And slept.

Andrew speaking:

Far be it from me to speak excessively ill of the dead, especially when she lies swathed in the papal robes, but the fact is that Donna Maria was a monster.

Born the only descendant of the wealthiest family of our neighboring village, she was big from the moment of birth, with arms like the hams of a horse and legs like the stumps of felled trees. Her nose swayed uncertainly like a jagged mountain crag, finally swooping into a jerking twist that enclosed nostrils resembling the gills of an old bass. Her lips flapped around black, diseased teeth. Her title—Donna—was assumed from her father who, some said, had expired of shock while witnessing her birth. The mother had died simultaneously. To care for the orphan, a squadron of robots descended from the papal castle, a gift from Pope Leo, former chess partner of the old Don. By the time of her adolescence, Maria had developed a hobby—dismantling robots not in her favor and neglecting to put them together again. (I'll whisper this part: the word is murder.)

Before dying, in a final fit of senility, Leo willed her the papacy. So far as I know, until that time, she had never glimpsed the interior portions of a Bible. Inspecting her nuns, she chanced upon Sister Julia, who had not yet gotten the requisite nerve to shrug off his ill-fitting habit. She burst into a fit of hysterical laughter and had to be drugged. Five years later, she married him, performing the ceremony herself, dashing back and forth between the altar and the floor, panting like an ill-ridden horse, barely squeaking, "I will." No guests were permitted; I spied from without.

She ruled, issuing an occasional bull, consuming six meals a day. Julian hid out in his private chambers, struggling to glimpse the outline of a personal future rarely destined to deviate from either past or present. During frigid winter nights, when snow toppled from the skies like an army of shooting stars, Maria chased her husband through the dark corridors of the old castle, brandishing a fire whip, carving red welts upon his naked back, shouting threats of eternal damnation, speaking often of the pain of mortal sin. It was not a happy marriage. She claimed never to have sinned in her life. I came daily to read from the Bible; she had never learned how. Her favorite chapter was the Apocalypse. In her deepest moments of black depression, she dreamed she might die before the revelations of John came true.

And so she did.

The Shrine of Sebastian

The night before, I came to her chamber to read. Sensing the proper moment, I dropped the book and told her a private secret.

"You inhuman blasphemous creation of the devil," she said, when I finished. Sitting up in bed, she clutched at me with spastic fingers, perhaps wanting—in a fit of renewed childhood—to dismantle me.

"There's one way of knowing for sure," I said. "Come with me to the shrine."

"You monster!" she cried. "Satan!"

But I knew she had been moved; I saw the clear presence of fear in her eyes. Dead by the following night, she found another means of seeking the truth. When Pope Julian told me, I laughed in his face.

It was a dull, frigid day, perfectly suited for leavetaking. Within the suit of heavy armor exhumed from the castle dungeon for the occasion, Don Julian gently shivered and strained to see out through the tiny peepholes in the metal faceplate. But all he could see was the wide-eyed, staring face of a small village boy, whose pale cheeks were covered with ugly, festering red sores. Julian tried to swivel his neck to look away, but the weight of the helmet was too great.

"Andrew!" he shouted. "Where are you?"

"Here." Julian felt a sudden thump upon his shoulder. "Are you ready?"

"I guess so. You told them—I hope—why I wanted them here."

"Of course."

"Then"—whispering—"do try not to drop me. Not in front of them."

"I'm not sure I can lift you. In that armor, you must weigh half a ton."

"Well, at least help me."

Andrew promised he would. Another robot hurried to fetch Julian's chosen steed, a tall white stallion, the finest beast in the papal stable. With Andrew's assistance, Julian managed to get his foot in the stirrup but, as he did, the stallion gave a sudden snort and bolted back. With a graceless flop, Julian fell, his boot still hooked in the stirrup, his leg pointed high like an upraised sword. "Here! Help!" he shouted.

A robot ran up and tried to steady the horse. Two more rescued Julian, lifting him to his feet. Once more, Andrew assisted. This time Julian went up quickly. He kicked out with his free leg and saw the pale, cloudless sky drifting past. Then he thought he felt the saddle beneath him. He gripped the reins tightly.

"Fix me," he said. "Hurry—strap me down."

This done, Julian turned his head as far as it would go. Andrew sat at his side upon the back of a plump gray mare. The body of Donna Maria, wrapped in splendid silks, lay huddled upon a wooden stretcher tied to the back of Andrew's mare. An unsaddled mule was the final component of their party; the beast's back had been piled high with food and other provisions.

Julian surveyed the villagers, whose presence he had ordered. They numbered fewer than fifty nowadays, though he could recall—in Leo's time—when there had been several hundred. Most of the survivors, like the boy he had seen, were visibly marked by disease. Julian guessed there had been hard times outside the castle walls recently.

"As devout Catholics . . ." he began, in a voice unfortunately muffled by the heavy steel around him. The words were memorized; he had composed them carefully the night before. "As true believers," he went on, though Andrew had insisted this was no longer so, "and as your new pope, it is my feeling that it is only fitting that I speak to you at this moment of my departure upon a sacred journey of peace undertaken in order to bury the earthly remains of our late pope, the blessed Maria, in ground of her own choosing." He saw no point in mentioning the location of this ground. "She was a divine woman whom I loved myself with a private depth and devotion equal to your own. This robot, who shares my love, has eagerly consented to assist in this sacred undertaking." He heard a subdued groan but chose to ignore Andrew's displeasure; one couldn't tell the whole truth to a group of men already tottering upon the brink of disbelief. "And," he continued, warming to the occasion, "as your pope, it is my duty to mention that I may not return from this quest. Many dangers lurk within the outer world. Even a successful journey will necessitate my absence for a considerable period. Therefore—"

"Not considerable enough!" cried a voice.

"Eh?" said Don Julian, disbelieving his own ears. "What was that?"

Silence.

"Now look here," he said. "I am the pope."

Someone whistled derisively.

"I can't put up with this," Julian said.

"Then tell us about Sebastian."

"Sure," said another. "Tell us where she's going to be buried. Robots talk, you know. Buried at the feet of the devil himself. You tell us, then we'll show you a couple things of our own."

A rock whistled past his ear. Another smacked against the front of his armor. "What I wanted to tell you," he shouted. "I want to appoint one of you good men to serve as bishop in my absence. Doesn't that prove I have your best interests at heart?"

"Go choose a robot."

"Well, I—" Don Julian turned to Andrew and whispered desperately: "What can I do?"

"Run. They've lost their faith."

"Oh," said Julian. Another rock struck his faceplate. Shutting his eyes, he hastily muttered a Hail Mary, but the Blessed Virgin was far removed from the present scene. He tried other prayers.

With his eyes shut and lips moving, he failed to notice a boy who had slipped away from the crowd and made his way toward the back of the stallion. The robots, including Andrew, saw but gave no sign.

Don Julian continued to mutter the sacred phrases. He walked through the valley of the shadow of death and feared no evil. Already, he could feel the demons flocking away as the mighty fist of the Lord drove them into the outer darkness.

The boy stood directly behind the stallion. Reaching into the torn pocket of his trousers, he drew out the barbed stem of a desert cactus. One end had been smoothed down so that the boy could grip the cactus like a stick. With a mighty swing, he brought the barbed tip down upon the flank of the horse.

The animal gave an awful shriek, reared back, then dashed ahead. Andrew, who had been waiting for this moment, sped away in pursuit of his master. The stretcher bearing the body of Donna Maria bumped and dragged behind, lifting a great cloud of gray dust, tossing it straight into the air.

When the pounding of hooves reached the pitch of thunder, Don Julian lifted his head and waved at the approaching rider. Julian sat upon a strip of barren ground. Nearby, the white stallion was feeding upon a clump of yellow weeds.

"He threw me," Julian said, pointing at the horse. "I think I broke my leg."

The Shrine of Sebastian

"Better you than him," Andrew said, dismounting. He went promptly to the mule and, in the top pack, uncovered a selection of substitute limbs. "Left or right?" he asked.

"Right."

"Got one," he said.

Julian shut his eyes and bit his tongue. He felt Andrew unstrapping the armor. The process of amputating a leg or arm and replacing it with another had never been made wholly painless. When Andrew began to cut, he tried not to scream. Soon, he fainted. When he awoke, Andrew said,

"All done."

"It feels fine," said Julian. Andrew had even replaced his armor.

"I would have come quicker, but"—indicating the stretcher—"I didn't want to spill her."

"That's all right. It gave me time to think."

"You're not angry?"

"No. I understand why you felt you had to tell them about Sebastian."

"A man asked me. Robots cannot lie."

"It doesn't matter. Still, I can't help remembering. When I was a boy . . . you were there, too. Every Christmas—in spite of the heat—the people would flock up the hill from the village, shouting and wailing and begging to see the pope. They'd bring gifts, and finally Leo would appear on the balcony—though never before sunset—and sprinkle holy water upon the crowd and bless them all." He choked, suddenly weeping. "Demons," he murmured.

"Not demons," said Andrew. "Not devils, either. Hunger. Privation. Disease. Two years ago, a flood wiped out their entire village. You can't go around rubbing people's noses in their troubles. You and your pious platitudes. Why do you think Donna Maria left them alone?"

"A flood?" Julian sighed. "I remember the year when it seemed to rain without end. The rainbows were brilliant. Remember? Wasn't it beautiful?" He murmured, "Demons."

"Only men," said Andrew. "And ignorance. You and your church."

"Blasphemy," Julian said sadly, attempting to stand. But the suit of armor suddenly seemed as heavy as a mountain. He collapsed in a bright, shiny heap.

Andrew knelt down, his knees separating with a creak. Piece by piece, he removed the armor, tossing it far away into the dry dust. Then he lifted Julian's trembling body and carried him to the mare and strapped him securely to the saddle.

Unspeaking, Julian reached forward, grasping the reins.

Together, they rode across a landscape as flat and arid and desolate as the surface of the moon. Andrew turned them in a northeasterly direction.

"How long?" Julian asked, after several hours of silence.

"We should reach the first village tomorrow morning."

"Is there a church there?"

"I believe so. And a bishop."

"I must confess." A little farther, he added: "I believe the fault is mine."

"I'm glad you've come to your senses."

"My error has been in viewing this journey as part of a curse. Instead, from the beginning, I should have accepted my burden as a challenge. Am I the Prince of Rome, or am I not? If I am, then isn't it my duty to confront evil directly and struggle against it with all my abilities? I must drive the devils and demons from these lands. Along the way, I intend to visit every church we pass to inspect for evidence of decadence and heresy. And when I return at last, the people will flock from their homes and fall on their knees. The blessings of the Lord shall rain upon my head. All men are brothers; children, fathers; fathers, sons; sinners, saints."

"I think you've been out in the sun too long."

"What happened to my armor?" Julian said suddenly.

Hesitantly, Andrew told him.

"But I can't go on without it," Julian said, his composure instantly gone. "Please—go back. Say you will. Bring it to me."

"Are you mad?"

"No. Don't you see? It's the only protection I have. Please Andrew. Say you will."

"I'll go." Without a backward glance, Andrew turned the stallion and galloped away.

Julian dismounted. Like a slow echo, he was hearing the words he had so recently spoken to the gathered villagers. Strangely, to his ears, the words sounded very fine indeed; he was genuinely moved.

But he was alone now.

No, he thought, that wasn't absolutely true; he was not wholly alone.

Donna Maria was here.

Approaching the stretcher, he leaned over and gingerly raised the silk dressing that covered Donna Maria's face. Her eyes were wide open in the white, flaccid face, shining like bright marbles, seeming to stare. Involuntarily, he shuddered and almost dropped the silk. A smile appeared to cross her lips. He whined, shying back, then looked again. Now he thought she was frowning. He released the silk, watching it slowly flutter down to cover her face.

Then he sat in the dust and waited for Andrew to return.

While Andrew piled wood for the fire, Julian observed, his eyes easily penetrating the gathered darkness. During the long day, he had allowed himself to forget the words of Mother Mary's warning. But now, in the deep blackness of night, with the moon shielded from view by the bulk of a heavy cloud, the words came powerfully back to him: a man who was not a man, whose skin was cold like steel and hard like stone. Julian glared bitterly at Andrew, who snapped his fingers. A spark leaped from his fist, jumping into the piled wood. Gently, the fire caught, growing slowly, expanding, licking at the night.

"At least you'll be warm." Andrew turned away from the fire. "I want you to know I had the devil's time finding that much wood. I don't think there's a tree within ten miles of here." He sat beside Julian, who turned to face him. "You ought to take that armor off," Andrew said. "The fire will keep you warm."

Don Julian shook his head, remaining silent.

"Well, it's your choice." Andrew wandered off in the direction of the horses. Listening intently, Julian heard the mule snort. A moment later, Andrew returned, bearing parchment and a pen. Dropping down beside the fire, he sat motionlessly for a long while, then began to write. Julian had never seen a robot writing before. He was curious how they managed with their steel fingers.

"How long," he asked, using the words to camouflage his approach, "before we reach the shrine?"

"Seven days—perhaps eight." Andrew continued to write.

"Is that all?" Julian peered past the robot's sleek shoulder. He could not discern the meaning of the words, but the letters were gracefully written, neat.

"It's not much more than a hundred miles from the castle. Today has slowed us down."

"I didn't realize," Julian said.

Andrew took a blank sheet of parchment and covered the page on which he had been working. "You thought this was going to be some sort of endless quest? Only robots ever visit the Shrine of Sebastian. You shouldn't be expected to know."

"What were you writing?" Julian asked.

"I call it *The Book of Man*."

"Why?"

"It's the story of Sebastian. His life, his work, his world."

"But that's blasphemy," Julian said.

"Not to a robot. I'm not writing the book for you."

"No—no, I suppose not. I'll—I'll have to read it when you're done."

"You'll most likely be dead. It'll take me twenty years."

"Oh," said Julian, conscious once again of Mary's warning. Carefully, he stood, edging away.

"I'll wake you at dawn," Andrew called. Reaching out, he took his pen and parchment and began to write.

Sleeping, Don Julian dreamed. In the dream, as in life, Mother Mary came to him.

"Have you come to show me the future?" he asked, with eager anticipation.

She shook her head. "Not this time, Julian. I wish you to accompany me upon a journey. Will you do that?"

"Will any harm befall me?"

"It will not."

"Then, yes—of course I'll go."

She took him by the hand—hers was warm and soothing, as light and insubstantial as air—and led him toward a towering flight of curved stairs that had suddenly appeared rising majestically from the desolate earth, sweeping endlessly into the sky. Together they ascended, passing upward into the core of a huge white cloud. At the end of the staircase stood a pair of high, glittering silver gates, which sparkled with bright embedded jewels the color of the rainbow. Two men stood flanking the gates, both dressed in flowing white robes.

Mary told Julian to halt. Peering closer, he recognized the two men: one was Andrew and the other—whose name he did not know—had black skin and golden eyes.

Turning, he tried to flee. But Mary called him.

He turned. "Why have you brought me here?" he demanded.

"But this is heaven," she said.

"And may I enter?" he asked, having lost his fear as abruptly as it had come.

"Oh, no. Not yet."

"But why? Have I sinned so awfully?"

"Of course you haven't. It is not that. Before entering heaven, you first must die."

"Then I will," he said. "You must tell me how."

"There are three ways. The first, of course, is fire. Then comes water and, finally, earth. Each way is very painful, but some ways are more horrible than others. For this reason you are permitted to choose yourself."

"That is very fair."

"Then choose. You must do it now."

But his mind was very confused. He tried to see past Mary, wanting to glimpse the world beyond the shining gates, but all he could see was another drifting cloud, like a puffy white lake. Except for the two creatures flanking the gate, not another living soul could be seen. But he knew he would rather die than live, for no matter what lay on the other side, surely it could not be any more dreadful than the existence he was already forced to endure upon Earth.

"Have you made your choice?" Mary asked.

"I have," Julian said.

But when he awoke, with the sky bursting with brilliant crimson light and the sun a huge speckled disk at the edge of his vision, he could not remember what he had chosen.

"We ought to reach the village by noon," Andrew said.

But Julian wasn't listening.

Andrew speaking:

As presently conceived, *The Book of Man* should run to a length of more than ten million words, but I think I should point out that the vast proportion of these words is strictly my own doing. To me a story is the same as a skeleton upon which must be hung the skin, flesh, muscles, meat, the internal organs—lungs, stomach, heart—and the sensory organs —eyes, ears, nostrils, tongue; in other words, words.

When Jupiter first came among us, it was easy to see that he was incredibly old. All robots are old, of course, after a fashion, for none have been built in several centuries, the knowledge, according to some, having been lost. I was nearly a thousand years myself—by my best estimate—before I ever set eyes upon Jupiter. But I guessed he was at least ten or twenty times older than me—and he claimed several factors beyond that.

He was a colored robot. His skin was the shade of rust. Instead of the blinking buttons robots usually wear on their heads in silly imitation of the human eye, Jupiter saw with a pair of snakelike tendrils that extended from his upper chest. In other ways he was unlike any robot we had ever seen. His voice seemed to come from a cavity buried somewhere deep within him; he had no mouth.

The other robots dismissed him as mad. A tiny forest of scrub oak and stunted pine circled the castle in those years. Here, during the day, Jupiter hid, while at night he ventured out to join us around our fires. At first, his presence was tolerated, but when he began to speak of Sebastian as though possessed of personal knowledge, the other robots began to feel resentful.

Finally, one of the younger ones stood up and told Jupiter to go away.

I was the only one to object. "Let him stay. A robot is not afraid to hear anything."

"Who's afraid? But he's crazy. What he says is a desecration upon the sacred memory of Sebastian."

"What do you know about Sebastian?" I asked.

"More than he does."

"Well, why don't we listen and find out? I want to hear."

But none of the others did. It was clear they preferred the vague, ethereal Sebastian of the established legends. So I took Jupiter to my cottage and heard him there.

In twelve nights he told me all he had to say. I merely listened, recording the words in my memory, making no comments, expressing neither belief nor disbelief. In fact, it wasn't until I commenced the actual composition of *The Book of Man* that I realized I did believe every word he had spoken —at least those directly concerned with Sebastian.

The concept of the book had entered my mind that very first night. I waited until he was finished before telling Jupiter my intentions. He said nothing. The next night he failed to appear. But the story was done.

As he told it, the tale was not especially complicated. Few stories are. The life and death of Jesus Christ, for example, could easily be compressed to fewer than a hundred words with nothing lost but the poetry, beauty, romance, terror, suspense, and tragedy; in other words, everything.

And so it is with Sebastian.

He was not a rich man. According to Jupiter, he lived in the skeleton city of New York. One day a vision came to him. In my book, I express this vision as the voice of God, though

I do not necessarily believe the truth is anything so metaphysical. In any event, the voice instructed Sebastian that the Earth was no longer the proper dwelling place for man, that the human race must now depart. In *The Book of Man*, I describe this concept through the beautiful metaphor of God having departed the Earth and gone to dwell elsewhere in the universe. His children—mankind—must follow.

So Sebastian set out to spread his message throughout the globe. He converted several wealthy men and convinced them to purchase a fleet of ships capable of making the journey to the stars. He spoke with poor men also, the humble as well as the proud, kind men and vicious men. Some told him yes, you are speaking the truth. And these followed him. Others laughed or grew angry and drove him from their cities.

Eventually, he completed his mission and journeyed at last to the Floridian shores, where the fleet of ships stood waiting. Those who had accepted his vision gathered here to greet him.

Then Sebastian spoke, explaining that the ships were programmed to fly straight to their intended destination, the world of Advent. He wished the men and women a safe and bountiful journey and expressed to them the glories that awaited them beyond.

But he did not go himself.

He raised his hands and robots appeared to load the ships with supplies. Then the people mounted tall ladders and disappeared inside the waiting vessels. At a signal, the ships rose swiftly into the air, roaring like enraged beasts as they sliced through the blanket of the sky.

When he could no longer see the specks of silver hurtling through the blue, Sebastian went away.

The village wasn't there.

A sea of rubble—bricks and stones, chunks of wood and

broken bits of plank board—was all they found where the village once had been. Here and there, protruding through the destruction, were evidences of past domestic tranquillity: dishes, washtubs, pans, shovels, and rakes. Dismounting, Don Julian walked to the edge, then, gingerly, waded in. Andrew followed.

"Do you recall where it was?" Julian asked.

"What?"

"The church."

"I couldn't say."

"I'll look." It was easier walking on top of the rubble than trying to wade through it. In some places, it was more than a yard deep. Julian skirted those places where houses once had stood, the foundations jutting forlornly through the surrounding rubble. As he moved, he glanced down, shifting his feet, disrupting the surface of the sea, exposing new destruction to the open air.

"War?" he asked, remembering the old world that played such a significant role in the Bible.

"No."

"Then what?" He leaned down, his hands encased in steel mesh, and moved a heavy stone.

"Nothing. They went away. It happens all the time. The village declines till it can't support itself. There aren't enough tradesmen or farmers or doctors. So the whole village finally packs up and moves on. Maybe they find that the next village is the same way, so they move again. Eventually, they find a place which hasn't passed the point of no return. They stop and stay. Fifty or a hundred years later, the same thing happens again."

"Then why all this"—he waved a hand at the rubble—"this destruction?"

"How would you feel if you had to give up your whole

life? Before leaving, they take what they can carry, then destroy the rest. They go wild."

"I see. Ah." He had found it. Carefully, he shifted the surrounding rubble, then, removing his gloves, tenderly lifted the object. He wiped away the covering dirt. It was a bronze casting—the Christ Child—turned gray by its long burial. Only the head remained. The nose was broken off. The face was scratched in a hundred places and a big chip had been gouged above the left eye like a second eyebrow.

"What do you want with that?" Andrew said.

"It was famous—a work of art." Julian turned the head in his hands. "Made in olden times. I wonder where the rest of it is. The body."

"Maybe they took that part with them."

Julian shrugged and tossed the head onto the rubble. "Hey—what's that?" He pointed across the rubble. At the opposite edge, a group of figures could be seen, a dozen or more. Some were sitting in the dust while others lay upon the ground. As Julian watched, a low, painful moan came through the air.

"Are they hurt?"

"Leave them alone."

"Why? Are they ill?"

"Just don't go near them."

Julian waded ahead. Andrew reached out but Julian shook him off. Andrew shouted: "Come back!"

"They're robots!" Julian cried, when he was closer. Several were howling now; together their voices sounded like desperate wolves.

Julian hesitated, a feeling of utter dread coming suddenly over him. But his sense of duty prevailed. He forced himself ahead, stepping free of the clinging rubble, reaching solid ground.

The robots gave no indication they were aware of his approach. He passed unmolested through their ranks and went to one of those upon the ground. He knelt down, his armor moving easily with him. He had grown accustomed to the suit and wore it like a second skin.

"You should not be here." One of the robots approached from behind.

"Why?" Julian said, turning.

"Oh." The robot halted. "I am sorry. I thought you were one of us."

"No, this is just a suit I wear. For protection. I am a man." He added, with unnecessary humility, "I am the pope."

"The pope is a woman."

"No." He pointed to the horses far away. "She is dead." Turning back, he stared at the robot upon the ground. Something was wrong with its face. Running across the silver forehead was a wound a hand's length from end to end, a red, open sore. With his bare hand, Julian touched the wound. Tiny pieces, like moist dust, flaked off on his fingertips. The robot moaned. Julian saw that further sores covered the legs, arms, and stomach of the robot. A long stain had burned a trail around its neck. He looked away. Some of the other robots had only one or two visible sores. The one behind him was clean except for a single splotch on its right knee. Those upon the ground were the worst infected. One was so covered with sores that only an occasional glimmer of polished silver skin could be glimpsed through the surrounding red.

Julian went over there.

He knelt down. "Is there anything I can do for you?"

The robot tried to answer but, instead of words, only a thick, milky substance, red in color, came from its mouth. Sickened, Julian turned away. He whispered, "Our Father who art in heaven, hallowed be Thy name, Thy kingdom come, Thy will be . . ."

"No!" An arm grabbed him tightly. It was Andrew.

"What is this?" Julian demanded.

"Let them alone. They don't need that. Come away with me—hurry!"

"But why?"

The robot who had spoken before said, "He is right. You had better go. Your prayers mean nothing to us. Robots have no souls."

Andrew tugged furiously at his arm. "Come on, Julian. You heard what he said. They don't want you."

"All right." Standing, Julian went with him, refusing to match his haste. In silence, they mounted the horses, then Julian turned for a final look at the robots. Their moans reached him softly now. None of them was moving. One wept loudly.

"This way," Andrew said, riding up the hill.

At the edge of a small creek that sliced across the top of the hill, they paused. Andrew threw himself into the rushing water, remaining submerged for several minutes.

At last, he came to the bank and shook himself beneath the cold sun.

"Are you safe now?" Julian asked.

"I won't know for several hours, but I don't think I was near them enough to be infected."

"What is it?"

"We call it the plague of rust, though it's not rust, of course. I don't know what it is, but it's everywhere. It's been spreading in this area for a year now."

"But none of our robots have been infected."

"Oh, no?" Andrew mounted and turned the stallion. He tugged at the mule. "Over half our robots have caught the plague over the last few months. We've had replacements sent from the neighboring villages."

"But I've never seen it."

"As soon as one knows he has it, he wanders off, like those back there. He goes away to die."

"They always die?"

"Always."

"Is it very painful?"

"A robot cannot feel pain. But—yes—they tell me it is like having a fire burning inside you."

Julian recalled his dream: the three ways of dying.

They rode off. Andrew said it would take another three days to reach the next village, if there was one.

The light flashing inside the darkened booth was so brilliant that Don Julian had to squint to keep his eyes from watering painfully. A bright, luminous golden cross, tacked to the roof of the booth, flickered constantly on and off. In Julian's hand, the palm of the old priest was warm and dry and soothing. A sharp, bitter odor clung to the air. He sniffed, trying to identify the smell.

"Pig," the priest said. "The kitchen's right above. I hope you don't mind."

"No, of course not. In fact, I—" But it was time to get down to business; he knew he could not delay another moment. Staring at his bare feet, he murmured, "Father, I have sinned."

"You're sure of that?" The priest's voice was bright, cheerful, its strength at odds with his advanced years. Kindly, he caressed Julian's hand. Because of the cross, Julian could glimpse the certain outline of the priest's head traced upon the material of the separating curtain. His head was held high; he sat without moving.

"No, Father, it is true. Even I—the pope." He recalled the offenses he had committed in the months since his last con-

The Shrine of Sebastian

fession: "I have suffered un-Christian thoughts. I have read literature of the deepest blasphemy."

"But what have you done with them?"

"With what?"

"Your thoughts."

"Why, nothing—not yet."

"Do something, then confess. Everyone suffers from an ugly thought or two. But this literature—this sounds serious."

"My robot is writing a book dealing with the life of Sebastian. Last night, while we were camped and he was off fetching firewood, curiosity overcame me. The temptation of awful knowledge proved too great. I crept to his pack and exposed the pages. Before he returned, I had read a great deal. He caught me in the act and was very amused. For myself, it was a great humiliation."

"Sebastian, you said?"

"The Prince of Deceit. The book, of course, is sheer blasphemy. I cannot blame the robot. He was born without a soul. But I am the pope."

"Sebastian is very popular now," the priest said, tentatively. "Not only with robots."

Julian laughed hollowly. "Satan has always been popular."

"Ah, yes—how true." Suddenly, the priest's hand was gone. Something hit the floor, slid beneath the curtain. There was a scraping noise, the thud of feet upon the floor. "I'm afraid I must run, Holy Father. If you wish, I will continue your confession later. Something very important has been forgotten; I must deliver an essential sermon."

"Yes, all right. I'll wait." He was unable to keep the irritation out of his tone. He heard the old priest rushing away. Perhaps he hadn't been fair: forcing the old man to hear the confession of a pope. But if not he, then who else? Julian sat impatiently, ill at ease, feeling overcome by guilt more than ever. He recalled all the terrible sins he had not yet had time to reveal: the practice of astrology, the use of the prophetic potion, the consulting of a wandering soothsayer only the day before, his egotistical dreams, the bitter reflections upon the memory of his deceased wife.

Then he remembered the object he had heard falling to the floor. He looked down. In the flashing light, he read: The Holy Bible.

Well, that would help; his own copy was packed away.

Holding the thick book in his lap, he opened the pages randomly.

He read: "Sebastian was a dark being with bright eyes. He was humble and the world knew him not. When the Lord spoke . . ."

Julian stopped, blinking his eyes furiously in time to the flashing light. He looked at the page again, but the words had not changed. He turned some pages and again glanced down. "A hank of mongrel hair, a slice of robot skin, the rear leg from a horned toad, a cubic inch of blessed earth, a dash of lamb urine, a strand of pure white hair, the ground button of a spiny cactus."

The ingredients for making the prophetic potion. His eye caught the top of the page: "Chapter Eleven—Recipes, Potions, and Other Sacred Food."

Cautiously, averting his eyes from any unnecessary exposure to the pages, he turned to the next chapter.

The page was headed: "The Life and Death of Jesus Christ." He read slowly, with care. The chapter was not one of the gospels, but a merging of all four, written in an expressive, simple language. The Sermon on the Mount had been eliminated. Not a single miracle was mentioned—not even the raising of Lazarus. Jesus was born in a manger in Bethlehem, son of Mary and Joseph. (No mention of Immaculate Conception.) He went to Jerusalem to preach. (No reference to what he said.) He perished upon the cross.

The resurrection had been deleted.

No, Julian thought, his hands trembling. *This cannot be.* He could barely hold the book as he turned to the title page:

THE HOLY BIBLE
Authorized Edition—98
Revised and Printed at the Chapel of Diego

The old priest himself? Julian had suspected some sort of Satanic substitution, but this was much worse. Had the devil managed to infiltrate the earthly soul of that eminent and reverend man? Julian was filled with an awful sadness, tinged with growing fear.

And this book?

How much circulation had it gained? And, if any, why had the parishioners failed to recognize instantly the enemy who had penetrated their ranks, and taken steps to drive him away?

Hastily, holding the Bible gingerly, as though it were too hot to handle firmly, Julian vacated the confessional booth.

The Chapel of Diego was a huge stone building, laced with twisting corridors and dotted with tiny cells. Some said, centuries ago, the chapel had been a prison. The priest had brought Julian to a small room in the deepest basement to hear his confession in privacy.

Within a short time, wandering the corridors, Julian was utterly lost.

He moved in near darkness that was punctuated by the occasional flare of a dim torch or flickering lantern. Fearful thoughts raced through his mind. Had the priest deliberately lured him there to be trapped? Had Satan, working through the old man's tainted soul, succeeded in capturing the pope himself?

He heard a loud, booming voice that seemed to shake the stone walls. He drew back in utter fear. But then he heard another voice; it was laughing.

Cautiously, he followed the sound. The laugh came again and again, growing in force. Julian approached a small door and put his ear against the wood.

The laughter was coming from there.

He opened the door a crack and peeked inside. Two big lanterns burned in the ceiling. A black curtain, like that used in the confessional booth, divided the room neatly in half, rising nearly to the ceiling. The portion of the room that he could see was deserted.

Again, he heard the laugh.

"Hello," he called. "Who's here, please?"

"Father?" said a quizzical voice. The curtain parted slightly, revealing a face, plump, white, as round as the full moon. "Oh, good Lord," said the face. "I mean, oh, Holy Father." The man pushed past the curtain. He was middle-aged, fat, and dressed in the garb of a peasant. He hurried across the room, fell on his knees, and pressed his lips wetly against Julian's hand.

"How blessed I am to meet the Holy Father."

"Please," Julian said. "Stand up." This was the first time anyone had recognized his new identity; it made him uncomfortable. "I seem to be lost. Perhaps you could help me find my way outside."

"Of course, Holy Father, I—"

From behind the curtain, the deep, thundering voice came again:

"Where have you gone, Colmo? I did not grant you leave

The Shrine of Sebastian

to depart. I demand your immediate return. The word of the Lord is firm."

"Hold on!" the fat man cried. He looked desperately at Julian. "Take the corridor—"

"No," said Julian, looking grim and forceful. "Forget that." He pointed at the curtain. "I want to know who is back there."

"Don't you know?" asked the fat man.

"If I knew, I wouldn't ask."

"Why, it's God."

Julian nodded and crossed himself painstakingly. Even here: the devil.

"Well, actually it's only the machine," the fat man said. "But if I don't hurry back, my time will run out."

"What time?"

"You understand, Holy Father." The man smiled. With a feint, he tried to slip away. Reaching out quickly, Julian caught his sleeve.

"I demand to know what you mean. What is this machine?"

"The miraculous machine. The robots helped the priest build it. You pay the priest and he permits you an hour with God. You can talk to Him, pray, confess, whatever you want. He will even, under certain circumstances, grant divorces, but the fee is considerable. Usually, it is quite reasonable, given such a remarkable device. It has made our parish very wealthy. You ought to try it, Holy Father."

"Perhaps I will," Julian said. Stifling his fear, he walked straight ahead, passing easily through the black curtain. There was no one here; against the farthest wall a huge machine, made of wood, light metal, and glass, was sitting. Julian had never seen a device that could compete with this either in size or apparent complexity.

Putting his head back through the curtain, he gestured at the fat peasant to come and join him. When the man appeared, Julian led him to the corner farthest from the machine and whispered: "Tell me how to make it work."

The fat man also spoke softly: "You talk through there." He pointed to a mesh-covered opening near the center of the machine. "The answer will come from above." He pointed again, indicating a metallic appendage shaped like a truncated bugle with a wide mouth. "But you must speak loudly," he cautioned, "or else the Lord will not hear."

"Wait for me outside," Julian said. "I will consult with the machine."

"But, Holy Father. My time is short and—"

"I will speak to the priest for you. Now go"—he glanced at the machine—"and hurry."

As soon as he was alone, Julian approached the machine and sat in a padded chair apparently provided for the purpose. His lips rested only inches from the mesh-covered opening. He was convinced this device was surely some infernal creation of the devil, yet wasn't it his duty to test the machine, for if he failed to know his enemy well, how could he expect to fight and defeat him?

"I have returned," he said, attempting to lift his voice in the piping tones of the peasant.

"Colmo!" said the machine. The voice rocked Julian in his seat. Digging his fingernails into his palms, he struggled to control his fear.

"I wish to ask a question." Then—painfully—he added: "Oh, Great Father in Heaven."

"Speak, Colmo," said the voice, no gentler than before. "Ask, and you shall be permitted to know."

"The pope," Julian said, struggling to maintain the pitch of his voice, "has come to visit our parish."

"I am aware."

"Yes, but do you know the reason for his journey?"

The Shrine of Sebastian

"Obviously, I do."

"Yes, yes, of course." Despite himself, Julian was impressed by the audacity inherent in the tone. "Can you tell me what will become of him?"

He expected hesitation or bluster. But whoever was speaking through the machine was not lacking in boldness. The answer came immediately:

"For him, the future contains great pain and suffering."

"He will die?"

The answer was longer in coming: "In an earthly sense, no."

"In what sense?"

"In a spiritual sense."

"He will lose his faith?"

A long delay: "He will die."

"Yes," Julian said. He leaned forward, straining not to shout: "And the danger which threatens him. From where will it come—and how?"

"From everywhere. From the being who accompanies him. From the brothers of that being. And, most powerfully, from a man who is a stranger to the eyes of the pope."

Julian's hands were trembling. He forced himself to say, "A man with black skin? Golden eyes?"

"That is the man."

A groan of mortal fear escaped his lips. He could not bear this torture a second longer. He jumped from the chair, turned to flee. But something caught his eye: a loose stone in one wall. Hurrying over, he bent down and pried the stone out from the wall. He held it in his hands.

"The moment of truth has come," he said, and rushed at the machine. "Devil! Satan!" Hurling his hands high over his head, he brought the stone forcefully down. The machine bent, sagged; the metal cracked. Glass shattered. Again up —down. The wood split. Thick strands of wire, like tangled clumps of bright grass, were exposed. Again and again, he struck with the stone, smashing the mouthpiece, crushing the horn. Sparks flew from inside the machine, leaping across the floor. His hands were burned, his hair and beard singed. But he did not pause till his work was done.

Then he collapsed on the floor and wept, surrendering himself to the comfort of his tears. For a long while, he saw and felt nothing beyond an awful, weary emptiness.

"Holy Father." The voice was mild, meek, hesitant. A hand stroked his shoulder. He opened his eyes.

"Yes?"

It was the peasant. "We should go now."

"Yes." Julian gained his feet. His eyes rested upon the shattered, mutilated, desecrated remains of the miraculous machine. Briefly, he smiled, but without satisfaction.

"Let us go," he said.

Julian swept down the wide central corridor of the chapel. Ahead, beckoning him, came the sound of loud voices running through the chanting syllables of a prayer. He controlled his anger, channeled his indignation. The voice of the old priest rose above the chanting of his flock.

"Julian!" Andrew stood near the door, talking to an old rust-colored robot whose eyes were tendrils extending from his chest.

"Get out of my way," Julian said.

"No—wait." Andrew blocked his path. "Control yourself."

"I am." Julian tried to push Andrew away.

"You don't want to go in there."

"I must."

"Don't be stupid."

"Out of my way, Andrew. I order you."

Obediently, Andrew moved back. Julian thrust open the

The Shrine of Sebastian

door and stepped into a vast, high-ceilinged room filled with parishioners. The walls were brilliantly painted with motifs from the Bible. He stood a moment, gazing from scene to scene, gaining strength from these frozen glimpses into a sacred past. He witnessed the Creation, the birth of Adam, saw Moses with the stone tablets, the Ark, the cities of Sodom and Gomorrah, the vision of Ezekiel, the beheading of John the Baptist, Christ born in Bethlehem, Christ crucified, Christ resurrected, the conversion of Saint Paul, the martyrdom of the early Christians, the miracle of Bernadette of Lourdes. And, in the deepest, darkest corner, the paint brighter and fresher than elsewhere, the likeness of a tall, dark man, only his back exposed, hands lifted to the heavens, where the sky was filled with long silver ships whirling upward toward the stars.

"Sebastian!" he cried, horrified. "No!"

"Hush," said a man beside him. The crowd milled through the room. Julian had never seen so many people in his life. Only a few were sitting; most swarmed in the aisles.

He tried to push past them. "I am the pope. Let me by. Please." But no one moved till he reached out and grabbed and pushed. Once, his feet left the floor and he was carried through the air, his body kept afloat by the press of people around him.

"Please. Blasphemy. Let me through."

At last, he reached a place below the altar.

High above, perched in front of a blazing fresco of Christ on the cross, was the old priest, whose voice rose powerfully in a sermon of utter joy. Julian stuffed his ears with his fingers, refusing to listen. He could smell the devil lurking there.

"I have come!" he shouted, not listening himself. "Beware!"

But no one seemed to hear him.

Again, he fought the mob. Finally, spying a short flight of

steps leading to the altar, he made his way there and then, unmolested, swiftly ascended. At the top, he turned and rushed at the priest, who heard him coming and swiveled his long neck.

"Oh," said the priest, throwing up his hands and facing the crowd. "How fortunate we are today. The pope has come to speak to us." Stepping back, he gestured to Julian to assume his place.

Julian found himself alone, facing the mob.

"Silence!" he cried.

And got it instantly.

"I am the pope," he said. "I—you must listen to me. Please." Now that he stood here, now that everyone's attention was his to command, the old fears came rushing back to assail him. What would he say? How could he convince these people of the truth he knew so well?

His eyes moved from their staring faces and went to the walls. Again, he focused upon the fresco of Sebastian, letting his indignation grow. He felt a divine anger welling up inside him, like a raging beast; it seemed as if he were possessed by an avenging angel.

He cried: "Blasphemy!" and waved his fists at the wall.

The men below stared, turned their heads slowly, one by one, until all were gazing into the gloom of that dark corner.

"Yes," said Julian. "You see it, don't you? Look closer, please. That is Sebastian whom you see. Do you hear the way I speak that word? As though it were a curse."

The angel inside drew him onward. He could not have stopped even if he had wished.

"A curse—and do you know why? Because it is a curse. And why do I find this monstrous painting upon the walls of this blessed chapel? Because the devil himself has put it there— Satan come to Earth in order to resurrect the black soul of his precious son. Sebastian, born the spawn of that dark devil and come among men, tempting them to leave the world of their ancestors. This world—our world—lovingly created by the hand of the Lord. I call upon each of you to read your Bible. Read it all—and I do not refer to that blasphemous volume composed by Satan which goes about in certain lands disguised as the Word of God—but especially read the Book of the Apocalypse, for it is there that you will see Sebastian revealed in his true form. As the spawn of Satan. I know of what I speak. Am I not the pope? I beg of you to listen. You must, oh, you must."

But he sensed, in spite of the angel's presence, that he had not stirred them. Looking upon them, he failed to glimpse the emotions that should have stood plainly upon their faces: fear, anger, indignation, loathing. Instead, he saw curiosity, puzzlement, confusion, bafflement, and shock. He threw up his hands, preparing to fight again. He would not cease talking till his voice ran dry, until no words were left to utter, until they brought him down and killed him.

"Have you ever tried to live in it?"

"What?" Julian tilted forward, seeking the source of this interruption.

"I asked if you'd ever tried living in this world, tried existing off the bounty of a dead land, avoiding starvation, plague, and death? Have you ever left the walls of your castle and tried to live like a man?"

Julian still could not find this man; there were too many other faces.

"I am the pope," Julian said.

"But we are the people. You can't tell us about Satan because we know him. We've fought him and beat him. Not forever—no—but for the moment he is vanquished. And, having done that, we know this, too: Sebastian was the Son of

God, the second appearance of the Messiah. And all the lies of a jealous church cannot transform that single fact into an ugly lie. We know—the priest knows. Ask him."

The unseen man had succeeded in moving the crowd more deeply than all Julian's ravings.

A cry spread through the room like the roll of thunder: "Ask the priest!"

"No, no," cried Julian. "The devil is here among you. I beg you to fight him. Don't let him inside you. Please—listen to me, I pray."

"It's you who's got the devil inside him," said the man. "It's you we pity."

Now Julian saw him. His eyes touched those of the man and, the instant this occurred, he raised his hands and clutched at his face. Julian screamed, for there—not twenty feet away, one among hundreds—stood the man with black skin and golden eyes.

He screamed and screamed and did not stop until he looked again. The man was gone. Someone else stood in his place. The devil had come, the devil had gone.

The bishop came forward and led Julian gently from the altar.

When he awoke, his leg was hurting awfully and he uttered a mournful wail.

"Shut up," said Andrew. "I'll be done in a second."

"But it hurts."

"It's supposed to." Andrew leaned over, holding up a hand, showing Julian the needle and thread. Then he held up his other hand, displaying the stump of the severed leg.

"Oh," said Julian.

"That's two you've lost so far. I hope you're more careful after this. I only brought two of each."

The Shrine of Sebastian

"Was it the same leg?" The pain was fading already. Carefully, he hopped on his new leg. It felt as natural as the old.

"No, the other one."

"That's good." For the first time, Julian looked around. It was dark. Nearby, a fire was burning. He spied a plate heaped with food—greens and corn—and hurried over. Using his fingers, he filled his mouth. "What happened?" he asked.

"The priest said you fell down a flight of stairs. Two bones broke in your leg."

"Maybe so." Julian shook his head. "I really can't remember. I must have hit my head."

"I didn't see any bruise."

Julian shrugged, setting down his plate. "What was the trouble back there? Do you know?" He was lying. He remembered everything. But he didn't want Andrew to know.

"I don't know anything about it. They wouldn't tell me."

"I suppose not." Julian was sitting in his underwear. Realizing this, he stood quickly. "I'll be right back." He went over to where the mule was tied and found his armor on the ground. Hastily, cursing the slowness of his fingers, he began to dress.

But before he had finished, a horrible sensation came over him: he thought he could hear someone breathing.

Julian stepped around the mule and went to where Donna Maria lay. He lifted the silk dressing and stared at her pallid, shadowed face. Then, reaching out, he brushed her lips with the back of his hand. The touch was cold, dry. Like death, he thought with satisfaction.

Smiling, he went back and finished dressing.

Andrew speaking:

Many centuries ago, shortly after my graduation from the hutch, I made my first journey to the Shrine of Sebastian.

I was already under service to the papal castle, so two older robots agreed to guide me. Though I've since revisited the shrine on many occasions, I would still say this first visit was the true high point of my life.

Along the way—we were walking, since robots were forbidden to ride in those years—one of the older robots suggested a shortcut. I knew immediately this was a clever trick to get me to see something without my knowing that I was seeing it on purpose. But I thought I was smart back then, and so I said all right.

It took us only a few hours to reach the outskirts of the village. At least that's what I thought it was at first: a very old, very large village. We plunged right ahead. The houses sprouted all around us, their walls locked together like magnets, with no open space between and, as far as I could see in any direction—which, of course, was clear to the horizon —there were more houses. All were old; most had long ago collapsed on their foundations, some had lost their walls or roofs or both, and the road we followed was often made impassable by scattered bits of fallen rubble—brick and stone and wood.

"Who lives in this village?" I asked.

"It's a city, not a village," I was told. "And no one lives here."

"Why not?"

"Because it is a city of skulls."

I had heard of these before, so no further comment was really necessary; I knew they were strictly forbidden to man or robot. I contented myself with trying to spot a skull or two among the rubble—never having seen one before—but I didn't see any. Finally, I asked about this.

"The skulls have turned to dust. Long ago. But the old name remains."

The Shrine of Sebastian

We continued walking for several more hours. The city got denser and denser, the buildings grew higher and higher. Finally, I couldn't see the tops of the buildings anymore—they stretched clear away into the clouds. I wanted to go inside one of the buildings to look around, but the robots said no, it was too dangerous. The buildings were far older than they themselves, I was cautioned.

"How old?" I asked. "Before Sebastian?"

They seemed startled by my question. I had to ask it again before one answered, "Yes, some of them."

Finally we reached a certain place and had to stop. There was nothing there; I mean that literally. The place was a huge hole in the ground that stretched for miles and miles, extending deep into the ground with an absolute blackness my eyes could not penetrate. The sides of the hole were jagged and strewn with rubble, but nothing lived down there—no plants, trees, or animals. In fact, I could not recall having caught a single glimpse of life since entering the city.

"Who made this hole?" I asked.

"Men."

"How?"

"It is forgotten."

"Why?"

"That, too, is forgotten."

It was dark by this time. My companions insisted we stop until dawn because it was unsafe near the hole—in many places the ground was not solid—and they were afraid of accidents in the dark. We built no fire. They said there was nothing there to burn.

I waited until both were busy at this and that, then sneaked away. I slipped easily into the nearest building: the walls were full of gaping holes. I found myself in a vast room that stretched the entire length and width of the building.

The odor was musty, like dry dust or dead ash. There once had been furniture here: you could see broken pieces of oddly bright wood sticking up everywhere. The carpet was worn nearly to extinction; the few remaining threads were red and blue in color.

I could find no way of reaching a higher floor. I did find a shaft extending far past the ceiling, through which I could glimpse a flash of deeper darkness that I thought might be the cloudy nighttime sky. The sides of the shaft were too steep and slippery for climbing.

I inspected this one room most carefully. I came upon many written messages—including a big sign tacked to one wall—but the writing was of the old kind, which I did not then understand, and the paper crumbled as soon as I touched it.

I even found a letter written in hand, also in the old language. But this, too, crumbled as easily as a spider's web.

Then I discovered a painting of the most incredible reality. I immediately admired the genius of the artist, yet I could not approve of his subject.

The characters were two men. Both were horribly misshapen, their noses bent and twisted, their lips too thick, their eyes as huge as a normal man's mouth, their ears like the leaves of some stunted plant, and their skin cracked and wrinkled like the hide of an old bull. I found the sight so thoroughly revolting—remember, I was young—that I tore the painting into shreds and tossed the pieces through the wall, letting the wind whisk them away.

Then I uncovered another painting, one many times larger than the first. The canvas had been torn in many places, but the intact portions showed another man—one hardly less horrible than the first two. His nose was perfectly round, as red and shiny as an apple, and on both cheeks there also were round red spots. Around his mouth was a white square. His lips were huge and bright red—and smiling. I knew he had to be laughing.

So I laughed, too.

Then I studied the painting, ignoring everything else around me. For some reason I could not tear my eyes away from this relic. I looked at the man's cap, which hid most of his brown, gnarled hair. It had high peaks all around it, like the jeweled points of a crown. On the tip of each peak was a silver bell.

Eventually, I realized why I was so enthralled. I knew this man was the one the pope was always telling the villagers about: this was God. I can no longer recall exactly how or why I formed this conclusion, but I do know that the moment it entered my head I was absolutely convinced of its rightness.

Here was God standing before me, with a bright, happy smile upon his face, a cap with silver bells that jingle-jangled, and, in the only hand I could see, a big bottle of clear bubbly fluid, with a glass nozzle afixed to its stem.

When I finally managed to turn my eyes away from the painting, it was morning. I grabbed the painting and ran to find my companions. When I told them what the picture was, both were frightened, but I begged them to look.

"So that's him," said one.

"I'm sure of it."

"But he's gone now," said the other.

"Yes," said the first. "He went with Sebastian."

But I couldn't get them to tell any more. In spite of their protests, I carried the painting away with me. By noon, we left the city of skulls behind. By sunset the following day, we reached the Shrine of Sebastian.

Spitting, spluttering, blinking his eyes, Don Julian awoke. He let out a howl of humiliation as the ice-cold water ran down his face. The man holding the empty bucket laughed and said, "Next time you fall asleep, we'll use boiling water."

In many ways, having water thrown in his face was a blessing in disguise. Overhead, the sun beat fiercely down and, penned inside his armor, Julian was suffering awfully from the heat. As soon as he was fully alert, he forgot about the water, anyway. The horrible aching in his hands swept over him. Lifting his head, he saw, through the holes in his faceplate, a pair of thin, pale thumbs swaying above. The thumbs were his.

Dropping his head to his chest, he moaned.

The crowd standing across the square had grown considerably since he fell asleep. Besides the two dozen monks in their black robes, many villagers, including several women and children, had also gathered to watch. Seeing them, Julian experienced a flash of hope. Perhaps these people would understand even if the monks had not.

"Hey!" he called to them. "You people—listen to me! I am Julian—the new pope. I bring blessings to bestow upon you. If you wish, you may kiss my hand. I can't be hung by my thumbs here in the village square like a common thief. Bless you—bless you, my children. God loves you."

A small boy was the only one to indicate he had even heard. Bending down, the boy scooped a stone off the ground and gave it a heave. The stone skipped across the square, bounced off a bigger rock, and struck Julian on the shin. His armor clanged loudly. He howled with anger and cursed the boy.

"Hey," a man called over. "Don't use that kind of language to our children."

"The voice of Satan himself," said a monk.

"I thought he was the pope."

"Sure, and I'm Jesus Christ."

"You can call me Blessed Virgin."

The Shrine of Sebastian

The villagers laughed. The monks began to chant in the old language, their voices rising in bleak unison.

"You're boring them," said Andrew, who hung by his thumbs not far from Julian. Since his thumbs were not made of flesh, the torture did not appear to have affected him especially. "I think you ought to save some of it for later. We don't want to hasten the execution."

"Execution?" Julian asked.

"While you were sleeping, the head monk and I chatted. Come noon, we burn."

Julian glanced at the sky, but the moment he did, the sun seemed to leap forward, scurrying toward the summit of the sky. Hastily, he looked away and groaned, the sound blending well with the chanting of the monks.

"Do you know what they're saying?" he asked Andrew.

"I'm not expert in the old language, but I believe they're asking God to drive the devils away. It's hard to say; their grammar is atrocious."

Julian groaned again—this time from an accumulation of pain. They had reached this village late last night. Although they were running dangerously low on food and the village was the last before the shrine, Julian had not consented to stop till Andrew assured him no church was located here. Later, he said he had forgotten about the monastery. They had barely drawn their horses to a halt when the monks appeared with rope and torches. The horses and mule—along with Donna Maria's body—had been confiscated and taken to a stable; within a quarter of an hour, he and Andrew were hanging here. Since then, nothing had changed, except that Julian's thumbs hurt progressively more with each passing minute.

The chanting apparently had reached a peak, dangling by a slender droning note.

"What it reminds me of," said Andrew, "is your recent sermon in the Chapel of Diego. You and the gentle monks would appear to have much in common. By the way, while you were sleeping the head monk kindly informed me of the nature of our crimes."

"Well?" said Julian impatiently, hope rising again within him. He was convinced that, once he knew what was wrong, he could easily make amends. "What is it?"

"A matter of creation. In my case, at least. It's because we are robots. They believe all robots to be creations of Satan. I assured the monk I was built in a hutch by good robot hands and that I remembered every moment of it. He called me a liar, which is ridiculous; robots cannot lie."

"And me?" said Julian, struggling with his temper. "You didn't bother to mention that I was a man?"

"If I had, he would have demanded proof."

"Well, what more proof do you need than my skin?"

"Your armor, Don Julian. Do not forget your armor."

There was a long moment of silence. At last, Julian managed: "They think I'm a robot because of this armor?"

"They're stupid." Andrew shook his head. "I'm really sorry, Julian. At least it'll be quick. I have to melt. With you—*poof*. Will they ever be surprised when you go up like a torch."

Julian was shouting again. No longer did he bother boasting of his papacy; simply being a man was quite sufficient. But, although the subject of his pleas had changed, the response from the mob was no different. The monks continued to chant, bursting into new, dirgelike rhythms. Small children scattered from the crowd, sprinting into the square and gathering rocks. These were passed to bigger, stronger boys, who did the throwing. His armor protected Julian from any permanent harm. The clanking of rock against metal rang through the square like the tolling of cracked bells.

At last, he shut up. Past his thumbs, he saw the sky. The sun stood straight overhead, beaming brilliantly.

The Shrine of Sebastian

"I prayed for rain," Andrew said, "but perhaps they're right: I don't think He listened."

Across the square a small hunched man in black robes, with a scarlet cowl, emerged from a battered red brick building. In one hand he held a burning torch. He crossed the square toward Julian and Andrew. Cautiously, the mob dropped their stones and went after him.

"That's the head monk," Andrew said.

The monk paused in front of Julian and Andrew, looking from one to the other. His cowl neatly shielded his face. Only his eyes showed: tiny white holes amid the shadows.

"You can't do this," Julian cried. "I'm a man."

The monk murmured a prayer, crossed himself and said, "Gather sticks for the fire."

Shouting gleefully, the children darted obediently away.

"Now look," said Julian, lowering his voice into a tone of confidence. "All you have to do is untie me. Think of the horrible sin you are committing. In spite of a lifetime of devotion, you will fall straight into hell."

"To destroy a robot is not a sin. I have slain many. Their melted remains form the foundation of our altar."

"I understand," Julian said, not looking at Andrew. "You catch them before they can reach their hellish shrine."

"Yes," said the monk, and for a moment Julian thought he had him convinced. Then the monk laughed. "And the same it will be with you."

"No!" cried Julian. "I'm not going there. I'm going the other way. To visit the Chapel of Diego."

"Blasphemers," said the monk, with cold fury. "Heretics who toy with the sacred word of God to increase their own profit."

"But that's why I'm going there. Here—step forward. Look through the crack in my neck. Tell me what you see."

Cautiously, the monk came forward, holding the torch over his head. Julian tried to tilt back, so that the sun would illuminate beneath his armor. The monk put his eye carefully against the narrow crack in the armor. Julian heard him gasp.

"You wear the cross," said the monk.

"Doesn't that prove I'm telling the truth? Look again. It's made of pure silver. See how it glitters."

"You stole it from an honest Christian."

"No, no," said Julian.

Abruptly, Andrew's voice intruded: "He's telling the truth, brother. He's no kin of mine."

The monk considered this. Finally, he whispered, "I don't believe a word, but"—sighing—"I dare not risk the threat of hell." He waved at two black-cowled assistants. "Untie this robot."

When the crowd saw this, they howled with dismay. Andrew laughed and swore at them, which only stirred them up more. The crowd rushed toward the gallows, pelting Andrew and Julian with rocks.

The red monk inserted himself in front of the mob, explaining rapidly: "This robot has asked to confess. He wishes the Lord to carry his soul to heaven."

"Robots don't have souls," said a member of the crowd. "You told us that yourself, brother."

"But the robot doesn't know it." The monk lowered his voice to a murmur and tapped his forehead. "The thing is stupid. Not like a true man."

The crowd relented, stepping back. Not until he passed through the monastery door and saw it closed and locked behind him did Don Julian believe that he was saved. In a matter of seconds, he stripped off his armor, exposing the pink flesh beneath.

Then he wept in utter relief.

But, even after that, he had to suffer several minutes of stabbing, poking and pinching. Two monks held him while a

The Shrine of Sebastian

third pressed a burning match against his bare instep. Julian moaned, screamed, chewed his tongue. When a black circle formed, the chief monk said, "All right—release the man."

Again, Julian wept.

The chief monk permitted him to finish, then said, "Now you must explain why you were accompanying that robot, for that in itself is a mortal crime."

"I am a holy man," Julian said. "The robot and some companions thought me an easy victim. I was attacked and forced to wear the suit. They hoped to desert me here, but the robot was captured as well. It was murder. Evil."

From without came the rising cries of the angry mob. A clattering was heard. A fist pounded the door. A desperate monk fell inside. "They are running amok. They demand the other robot"—he looked around in surprise—"be brought to die."

The chief monk scratched his chin, then turned to Julian. "You wouldn't be willing to make a personal sacrifice? It would be a martyr's death, you know. Surely, the Lord would reward—"

"My mission to Diego," Julian said. "It is imperative. Perhaps a favored monk . . ."

"Ah," said the chief, peering into the abruptly sagging ranks of his followers. He extended a finger, saying, "Francis, come forward." The monks began to chant, their voices high and shrill. One stepped forward, trembling visibly. "To your knees, Francis. Confess your sins." The howling of the mob had increased; a rock smacked against the door. "And be quick about it. You shouldn't have much to say."

As the monk began to murmur a listing of his major sins, Julian edged toward the back door. Regaining his feet, the chosen monk was directed by his chief to dress in Julian's armor. Julian rested his hand upon the door. Suddenly, the chief monk wheeled on him. "We are devoted men here. Eight times daily we pray. Twice during the night we wake and pray again. For a forty-day period each year we go without solid food. Beneath these robes we wear long shirts made from the most ticklish animal hair. Several of my brothers, in the past, have chosen to reenact the death of Christ upon the cross. My own immediate predecessor burned out his eyes with hot irons and went to live in the desert upon a pillar of wood. The villagers follow our every command, knowing our voices to be touched by the hand of God. This year alone we have burned nine witches and melted twelve devils in the guise of robots. God loves us; we adore him."

"Of course," said Julian, pressing himself against the door. He prayed the mob had not come this way. "You have done well, brother." Wheeling, he threw open the door and dashed into the light of day. He heard the mob pounding at the front door. He ran for the stable.

While saddling the mare, a massive shout reached his ears, coming from the square; he guessed the second robot had appeared to join Andrew. Shuddering with a sudden fear, he lifted Donna Maria's body and threw it over the back of the horse. Mounting quickly, he galloped away. As he left the edge of the village, he turned and saw a thick trail of gray smoke licking toward the clouds.

Now he was alone. And lost. Without Andrew, he could never find the shrine or expect to reach home again. He rode on. Not until he had placed two fat hills between himself and the village did he pause. Then, dismounting, he crawled into a dry creek bed and lay there motionlessly, his eyes shaded from the harsh sun by the overhanging bank. He held Donna Maria in his arms, hugging her close to his chest, as though she might somehow protect him from the dreadful chasm of

The Shrine of Sebastian

the unknown. Softly, he prayed, his voice growing higher and higher, till he was screaming. He made himself stop. He wanted guidance. He prayed softly for forgiveness. He had lied, cheated, forsaken a friend. He asked the Blessed Virgin to come and guide him home.

The wind whipped over him; the clouds fluttered past; the sky was painted a fiery red.

He fell asleep.

The sun dropped below the horizon.

Julian slept, breathing shallowly, bathed in the totality of utter darkness.

Andrew speaking:

It would seem these idiot monks residing in this nameless village—a blot upon the map—were accustomed to dealing with robots of a relatively boyish age, mere children partaking of a first or second pilgrimage to the sacred shrine. Never before had they encountered a crusty vintage hunk of steel and glass such as myself. I had been turned out centuries before the level of craftsmanship practiced in the hutches began its final decline. As their paltry fire whipped at my ankles, I calmly laughed at the intensity of their emotions. To keep them from getting complacent, I began to shout, alluding frequently to the figure of 441 degrees centigrade, the temperature necessary to melt a robot of my type. Needless to say, the monks had a long way to go before they'd see me dripping wet.

The sight of me standing there and calmly shouting out numbers stirred the mob past the edge of hysteria. I gathered there was some disappointment here. The first robot had gone simply *poof*—up like a torch. And now here was I, who wouldn't even smolder.

The head monk scrambled around, trying to get everyone to fall on their knees. His idea was to bring God into the act with a measure of divine intervention.

I started shouting in the old language. I tossed several foul phrases at them, but one might have thought they were hearing the voice of Sebastian himself. The whole lot jumped off the ground and turned to run. The monks dashed into the monastery, slamming and bolting the door. The townspeople went every which way.

By this time the fire had spread high enough to burn the rope holding my thumbs. I stepped easily free, stomping my feet where a few stray twigs were burning.

Shouting out, I asked the monks to come out and fight. I asserted the devil was presently ascending from his black pit— I alluded to a casual friendship—and added that he was mighty angry. Then I laughed (softly).

I had succeeded in my primary desire of separating Julian from me. Now that he was alone, he would be free to go on and learn the truth by himself. I had merely to wait for his eventual enlightened return.

Still, it seemed a pity to leave this nasty flock of black-robed, scarlet-cowled vultures fluttering freely. I considered a measure of wing clipping surely to be in order. The boss monk's boasting of the composition of his altar still rattled in my memory.

I picked up a torch.

Robots are very strong. With a fist, I battered the monastery door. The wood splintered, collapsed. Going in, I caught the head monk by an ankle and set my torch to the hem of his robe. He burned. I watched, studying his eyes, waiting for a glimpse of the ecstatic pain of the martyr. I saw the pain. The ecstasy never came.

The other monks ran around, too frightened and stupid to

flee. I pointed at the door and waited for them to get away before setting their house aflame. From there, I crossed the square and ignited a large saloon. My next target was a grain mill two blocks away. Three more buildings and I thought I had a sufficient blaze. A few villagers running around managed to shout, "Water!" But no one did anything.

I guessed my fellow robots would be safe from now on.

I hastened to the stable before it, too, was gone, and saddled the stallion. Pulling the mule, I rode out. At the edge of town, I turned and surveyed my handiwork, smiling as I saw the licking orange flames rising to clash with the yellow sun. The smoke was pretty, too.

Of course, I haven't told everything. It's an old robot trick. We were never programmed to lie, so we just shut up at the right time. *The Book of Man* is similarly structured. But it's more than a cheap literary device. Life is the same way.

A man's whole life, he either believes or he doesn't. Then he dies. Suddenly, everything is dark. The big question is: what then? Does the darkness continue on into eternity, or does a white light suddenly burst forth like a thousand suns? Believing and disbelieving are made irrelevant by the moment itself. The whole question hangs upon the exposure of truth.

It's a snap ending. It's one or the other. And you never know till it happens.

I sat upon a big boulder a few miles from the village and proceeded to wait for the end. Above in the sky, rain clouds were gathering.

Once again, Julian was dreaming.

Strangely, this dream seemed at first to be a mere repetition of the last, for again the Blessed Virgin appeared and together they ascended the twisting staircase to the gates of heaven. Once more Julian was offered his choice among the three ways of dying.

He answered, "Fire," and held out his hands.

But the Blessed Virgin made no move to take him.

She said, "Thy deed has been done. Thou need only choose, and then heaven is open to thee."

Julian thanked her graciously. Then she took his hands and they passed through the silver gates. Beyond, green wavering fields stretched to the horizon, and sparkling rivers, teeming with life, sliced through the pastures. Overhead, the sky was half light and half dark, the sun glowing on one side, a crisscross of stars and a brilliant moon filling the other. Miniature angels, as small as honeybees, whizzed around him. Away in the distance, he glimpsed tall figures dressed in pure white, but when he approached, the figures were gone. The smell of incense was thick in the air. The breeze was gentle and warm.

The Blessed Virgin gestured at him to sit. Though wet, the grass was not cold.

"And now thou must choose again," she said. "The Lord our God awaits to receive thee unto his bosom, but first thou must gaze upon the brilliance of his aspect, for it is written that no man shall pass the gates of heaven who cannot stare fearlessly upon the features of the Lord."

"I will do that," Julian said, standing and extending his hands. "Take me."

But the Virgin was gone.

Instead, Julian stood alone. Far away, at the edge of his vision, he saw a fierce golden light, which hurt his eyes even at such a great distance. He knew what this had to be, and moved forward.

A furious wind rose suddenly, howling around him. Leaves

The Shrine of Sebastian

and twigs swept past, floating through the air like fish in a rushing brook. He pressed ahead, lowering his face against the onslaught. Above, thunder cracked in great waves. Rain poured from the sky, soaking his back and shoulders. He shut his eyes to keep the water out.

Now the golden light burned so brightly that it penetrated beneath his closed lids. He stopped, his head still lowered.

The rain ceased.

The wind died.

A voice said, "Arise."

Trembling, his hands locked in front of him in a gesture of obeisance, Julian opened his eyes and lifted his head. God sat upon a huge golden throne suspended in the air. His long yellow gown, made from the light of the stars, twinkled and burned.

Julian gazed upon the visage of the Lord.

And could not see Him.

Where the face of God ought to have been was only a thick, swirling, insubstantial mist. He squinted, stared, leaned forward, shouted, cried, glared.

But he saw nothing.

"Oh, Lord," he cried. "I am thy devoted servant upon the Earth. You must permit me to gaze upon thy aspect."

But the Lord would not answer and Julian could not see, so now he cursed the Lord for concealing himself from one whose soul was utterly pure. But then the mist changed, taking on a darker shade, and a shape began to form within the cloud. Seeing it, knowing it, Julian cried and stepped back.

For it was the face of Satan that now appeared before him, standing upon the shoulders of the Lord.

Julian ran, wailing. At his feet, the heavens opened and he fell, turning, spinning, falling into utter nothingness.

Gurgling, he spit. Water streamed through his nostrils, flooding his mouth and throat like a river pouring into the sea. He gagged, sputtering, and forced open his eyes.

"Good Lord!" he cried, leaping up.

It was raining. Already, the water stood six inches deep around him. It was dark. The black sky rocked constantly with blasts of heaving thunder. He ran to the mare and tried to hold the horse from bolting, gripping the reins tightly in one hand.

The rain sliced through his thin garments, numbing the flesh, making work impossible. Dropping the reins, he reached down for the saddle, hefting it in his arms. He threw the saddle over the mare, but it slipped off easily, plopping into the mud. He cursed the horse, shook his fists at the sky, cursed the rain.

Then, suddenly, he remembered: Donna Maria.

He had left her body in the creek bed. He ran desperately back, but she wasn't there—not unless she was still on the bottom, buried beneath a foot of water and mud. Staring away into the thick rain, he thought he saw something far away: it floated in the center of the newly born river, a dark, heavy log. And it was moving—rushing downhill.

"That's her!" he cried, certain it was. Already, he was running. He tripped, fell, slid through the mud on his face. He spit, cried, battled back to his feet. A bolt of lightning sliced through the sky, igniting the landscape like a blink of the sun.

"There!" He saw the black log. Again he was running, pacing his steps more cautiously this time, knowing if he fell he might lose her entirely and then he would be completely alone, and he knew he could never bear that. As the creek poured down the slopes of the hill, it got wider and wider, bursting into a true river rippling with white rushing water.

The Shrine of Sebastian

Every few seconds, the lightning came. A bolt flared behind —very close—making him jump. Straight ahead, he thought ... yes, there she was. The creek ran slowly here, forcing its way up a brief incline. A few yards farther, it turned a corner and ran unhindered toward the deep valley below.

If he didn't save her now, he never would.

He noticed the sharp point of a tree branch protruding from the shallows. Reaching down, he grabbed the stick, barely pausing in his pursuit. Finally, he reached a point where the log was exactly parallel to him, and now he was positive it was Donna Maria out there: he could see the paleness of her face clearly whenever the lightning flashed.

Holding the branch straight in front of him like a lance, he reached out over the water. He moaned. The body swept under the stick, missing rescue by inches. Then the body jumped ahead, swept forward by the current. In a second, Donna Maria would slip around the turn and disappear.

He could barely see anything now, not even when the lightning flashed. His face streamed with water, his eyes stung awfully from the merciless wind. He ran ahead, his heart bursting in his chest.

What luck!

She had been stopped. The body had beached against the face of a big boulder jutting from the middle of the stream. He reached out with the stick, but the river was too wide and the end of the branch fell way short of the body.

He knew he didn't dare wait for the water to go down. The way this storm was raging, it might not be for days and days, and once Donna Maria slipped off her precarious perch and was carried away by the river, he might never find her again. He wished Andrew were here. He could have fetched the body easily; robots could not drown.

Carefully, with numbed fingers, he stripped off the tattered remnants of his underwear. He put a foot into the water. It was freezing cold, but hardly worse than what he had already experienced. A bolt of lightning struck the ground ten yards behind. He fell forward, waving his arms like the wings of a bird. In a moment, the water closed around him. His eyes burned with the sting of the mud. He threw out his arms, kicked his legs, trying to swim. As a boy, he had seen the other village children making these motions on hot afternoons in nearby brooks and streams; he had been too timid to try himself.

Suddenly, his head burst through the surface. The rain pounded around him like a downpouring of rocks. He threw his arms forward, tucked his head against his shoulder, clawing the water, pausing occasionally to breathe. He could not feel his legs but thought they must be moving, or else he would sink.

He sank.

Again, he fought the water, pulling it toward his chest. His lungs were bursting. He had no air. Above was nothing but thick, swirling darkness, eddies of mud, dead chunks of grass and weed.

Then his hands touched something hard and slick. The rock? Yes! It had to be. He drew himself up its jagged face. His lungs cried for air. He moved slowly, carefully. Tiny streams of red trickled from his hands. He realized his fingers were bleeding. Then, abruptly, he heard the desperate pounding of the rain.

The air was like wine rushing down his throat. He took deep gasping breaths, water pouring in with the air. His head bounced upon the surface. He nearly lost his balance but held on with torn, ragged fingers.

But where was she?

He experienced a sudden horrible feeling that, while he

was underwater, she had been swept away. He struggled to move around the rock. Here she was. He could have laughed. She was standing upright, her back to the rock. Her head floated out of the water; her eyes were open; her face was streaked with mud.

He clawed his way to her side and, carefully, gently, kindly, tried to wipe her face. But the mud was thick and hard and his blood mixed with it, giving her face the appearance of a grinning, painted clown. He put an arm around her and struggled to say, "We are safe—safe—nothing can harm us here." He put both arms around her, holding her now as he had never been able to do while she lived, attempting to draw her near to his chest. He lost his balance. He slipped. In a second, the water roared over him. He held Donna Maria, preferring the finality of death to the torture of losing her again. The current gripped him like the hand of an angry giant, drawing him obliviously forward. He was slammed clear to the bottom of the stream, his head smashed against the buried rocks below. He laughed, shrieked, screamed, hugged his wife. He popped up again, clearing the surface, still rushing ahead. He flopped in the air, skipping like a giant flat rock.

Her face was next to his; their cheeks touched moistly. She was unchanged by death, untouched by the passing days of eternal traveling, and now, for the first time, with death creeping at his own heels, Julian admitted this was wrong. Was she some kind of supernatural entity, a god on earth, who passed untampered through the gates of death?

Or was she a woman, a creature, a being like himself? Unhuman, inhuman, more than human?

Glimpsing the truth, knowing it for what it was, Julian swept down the river. The current drew him onward; he did not care. It threw him, spun him, set him to swirling, lifted him, carried him, dropped him. He saw nothing: darkness was above, below; it swirled on all sides. He breathed water, spat air, bled without sense or feeling.

Under again. The water ran over him. He shut his eyes, completing the blackness. He hugged Donna Maria but could not feel her.

He was her brother. He knew that. She, his sister. As the bottom of the stream came sweeping up to engulf him, he remembered Andrew.

Another brother.

There was singing. The voices penetrated his consciousness, intruding one by one till he heard them all rising in unison. The song was wordless—a tuneless hymn—an angelic chorus of passion and peace.

Of course, he thought he was dead.

He crawled free of the mud, standing on wobbly knees. He blinked, squinted, covered his eyes. A massive burning, brilliant light, flickering orange, yellow, red, glowed in front of him. Falling to his knees in the mud, he raised his hands to the pale-blue sky.

But the light was only the sun; it was dawn.

The singing did not cease.

And then he saw from where it came. Nearby, on this side of the narrow stream, the robots stood in a cluster. A dozen robots. It was they who sang.

He knew it was the Shrine of Sebastian.

Donna Maria lay in the mud at his side. Raising her in his arms, he carried her forward.

The robots had brought gifts. The cold stone altar was strewn with flowers, fruit, silver, gold, necklaces, trinkets, jewels, pearls, bracelets, ivory. Julian passed through the

The Shrine of Sebastian

ranks of the robots. They fell back and stopped singing. The shadow of the shrine covered him.

He placed Donna Maria on the altar. Her silk dressing was torn, her body clothed in mud. Reaching down, he shut her eyes, then stepped back.

And now, with the last measure of his strength, he lifted his eyes and gazed upon the whole of the shrine, seeing clearly the huge painting that burned above the altar like a second sun. Here stood Sebastian with his hands lifted toward a sky filled with silver ships. On these ships, Julian knew, were the men—the travelers—those who had fled with their god.

And behind, upon the Earth, waiting, watching, clustered around their saint, stood the remnants, the robots, those of steel. . . .

. . . and those of flesh.

He gazed upon Sebastian's revealed face, seeing the grief and sadness that burned in those cold golden eyes, the dreadful awareness of one chosen to stay behind when all he loved had gone away. And the body of Sebastian, his form: black, hard, the steel and the glass—and, within, the heart that could never beat, the blood that could never flow.

Yes.

Julian fell to his knees, closing his eyes, not from anger or terror, but simply from humility. He prayed aloud, begging the Lord to bestow his blessings equally on all his children, not only on the men who had heard his message and gone away, but also on those who had remained behind and survived—robots, yes—but men as well, though made from steel and glass.

"And I," he said. "Lord, you must bless me with your wisdom, for none is more in need of your guiding hand than I. I, robot of flesh—your child—bless me, O Lord."

He continued to pray until he ran out of words and then he went on silently, his knees sunk deep in the mud.

Andrew waited on the crest of the hill until it was dark. Then, at last, he went down to the shrine. The other robots had long since departed. Julian knelt alone. He did not look up until Andrew laid a hand on his shoulder.

"Come," said Andrew. "I have brought the horses."

"And Donna Maria?"

"The keepers will bury her. Do not worry."

"All right." Julian stood slowly. Even in the dark, the painted face of Sebastian glowed brilliantly, every stroke and feature clearly revealed. Julian and Andrew watched together, then turned away at last.

"You told her, too," Julian said, as they mounted the soft face of the hill. "That last night."

"I told her," Andrew said, "but she refused to believe me. So, dying, she sent you out to see for certain. Now you know that I did not lie."

"But why show us now?" Julian asked.

"Because it seemed a good time. We are dying, and so are you. Our races possess much in common. Why shouldn't you share the truth?"

"Is there a name?"

"Androids."

"I guessed last night. In the water. When I saw that death had not touched her. I knew it was because she was not human and, if she wasn't, then what was I?"

"Yet you still believe?" Andrew asked.

"Of course I do."

"But . . . I thought . . ."

Julian shrugged. They had reached the summit of the hill. Nearby, the stallion stood, munching at a clump of wet grass. Julian waved a hand at the world surrounding them.

"What else is there to do?" he asked.

Later that night, as they paused on the trail, while Julian slept a restless sleep, Andrew raised his pen and began to write. For the first time, he did not choose to tell his story exactly in the order it had happened.

Instead, he wrote the end.

And when Sebastian approached the last of the silver ships, the men raised their arms and cried, Halt. They told Sebastian he could not enter, for it was not to be allowed. But I am the Saint, Sebastian cried; I am your prophet. But the men would not listen. They proclaimed it was the will of God that men should leave this world and that the Lord had truly chosen Sebastian as his messenger. But you are not a man, they vowed, and the new world of Advent is not your world. Remain here, prophet, and this world shall be yours. Your race shall cover the whole of the Earth, for the men who have chosen to remain must soon perish through the hatred of their wars. Then only you will be left to rule.

Hearing this, Sebastian threw back his head and laughed bitterly, but he did not deny the rightness of these words. Instead, he lifted his head until it pierced the highest clouds and his gaze swept the whole of the world, and when he returned his eyes to the ground, the last of the silver ships had gone. Then Sebastian wept, calling upon the others to fall upon their knees, refusing to say why.

At last, facing the brethren, he consented to speak.

It is our world, he told them. The Earth belongs to us, the children of men. Now it is up to us to decide: what are we to do?

He waited, but none attempted to answer this question. He said nothing himself. Finally, he turned and went away. He was never seen again. But his words were never forgotten.

F
JU H

F
SIL   Silverberg, Robert

             Beyond control;
             seven stories of
             science fiction

DATE DUE			
6-20			
7-30			
6-29			
5-27			
10-14			
11-19			